Tangleweed and Brine

DEIRDRE SULLIVAN

ILLUSTRATED BY KAREN VAUGHAN

Little Island

PRAISE FOR DEIRDRE SULLIVAN

'Deirdre Sullivan's writing is beguiling, bewitching and poetic. Her prose is almost dreamlike, reminiscent of Angela Carter.' – Juno Dawson, author of *The Gender Games*

'Witchy, eerie and beautiful. These thirteen fairytale retellings already feel like feminist classics.' – Claire Hennessy, author of *Like Other Girls*

'Sullivan's prose is delicate and masterful, but there's a belligerence to it as well – these stories demand that we go as deeply with our reading as she has in her writing – that we listen to the women at the heart of these stories, that we see the shadows beneath the trees.' – Dave Rudden, author of *Knights of the Borrowed Dark*

'Dark, intimate and poetic, these stunning feminist fairy tales give voice to the witches and the wicked queens and twist the familiar into something salty and seductive, offering a collection of stories you'll feel like you know in your bones.' – Moira Fowley-Doyle, author of *Spellbook of the Lost and Found*

'Deirdre Sullivan's terse and stark renditions of fairy tales in *Tangleweed and Brine* challenge us to rethink what the destinies of young women were in traditional fairy tales, and she spells out what they might really be in other times and settings. Sullivan's original stories are riveting and offer readers unusual perspectives on how to read fairy tales in times of conflict.' – Jack Zipes, author of *The Irresistible Fairy Tale: The Social and Cultural History of a Genre*

Tangleweed and Brine
First published in 2017 by
Little Island Books
7 Kenilworth Park
Dublin 6W
Ireland

ISBN: 978-1-910411-92-6

'The Woodcutter's Bride' was published under the title 'Seeing Red' in *Watching My Hands at Work – A Festschrift for Adrian Frazier* (Salmon Poetry 2013).

'Meet the Nameless Thing and Call it Friend' was published in a slightly different form online (www.makebelieve.ie 2015).

A British Library Cataloguing in Publication record for this book is available from the British Library.

Cover and illustrations by Karen Vaughan
Interior book design by Fidelma Slattery

Printed in Poland by L&C Printing

Little Island receives financial assistance from The Arts Council/An Chomhairle Ealaíon and the Arts Council of Northern Ireland

10 9 8 7 6 5 4 3 2 1

TANGLEWEED – For Ciara Banks, with leaves and roots and flowers
BRINE – For Suzanne. Seasalt, water, home
I'm grateful for you both
My chosen coven
Love

TANGLEWEED

Old stories new, you'll

venture where you will

BRINE

TANGLEWEED

Slippershod

When you were young you used to be immaculate. Immaculate. The house, the carpet, walls could be a mess, but never you. She'd plonk you in a bath. You'd kick your chubby legs, and watch them pinken. She'd clean you and she'd sing to you and tell you little stories so you wouldn't be afraid to be submerged. To be so close to drowning and not drown. *Women such as we,* your mother told you, *we feel things strongly and we always have. You need to choose to love, and love, not hate. Be gentle and be kind and be my daughter.*

You say that to yourself these days.

A lot.

Words are not truths. Your father said he loved you. He didn't, though. Not after she was gone. And there you were, alone inside a house. He'd go on business and he'd shut the door. You learned to feed yourself. To tidy up. To manage and make do till he came home.

When he returned, he'd open up the door, and you'd approach. Eagerly, with smiles, the first few times. Then slowly, like a dog that knows that legs are built to kick.

He'd look through you.

You'd cook him dinner and he'd chew the food.

He'd look through you.

You'd go to bed and it would be the same as when she vanished. You have been lonely since your mother died. She loved you. And she died. The love he had for you was just a product of his love for her and when that died some of him died as well.

You have her clothes. You keep them in the attic. They are lovely. Sometimes you catch her scent upon the air. A soft and dusty flutter. It eats at you, like moths upon a cloak.

It's hard to have a house all by yourself. But it is easier than the alternative. When he comes home with *her* you close your eyes. He holds her hand. They are already married. Her daughters, two tight replicas, are scowling. She lets them be. You're not a thing that matters. Part of the house. A chair. A spoon. A plate.

They need your room for one of her two daughters. You start to sleep upstairs beside the clothes. You build a pile of rags, all bunched together. Little birds make nests to live in. And you are small. You come up to their waists.

You are a woman. You are a woman the size of a child. They treat you like a thing. They talk about you when you're in the room. The only way they look at you is down. It must be hard they say. To be that way. They mean the way that you have been for ever. And you are just a girl inside a house.

Your mother shaped like you. Your father loved her. It is things like this that get you through. Your back hurts, scrubbing floors and hemming gowns. Your sisters (they are not your proper sisters) talk about the future, marriage, babies, gowns and balls and things that they will buy with all their wealth. Their dreams are tall rich men to do their bidding, whose arms are made of heavy golden coins. To wrap around their bodies, keep them safe. Money can be armour, if you have it.

You mop. You break the sticks. Stand on little stools to stir the pot. Sometimes when they remember you are there, they talk about you. Your life was ruined as soon as you came out, they tell you. They bet that you were cute, though, as a baby. When you were meant to be a little thing. *And was it easier, then, for your mother, did you just plop right out, as though an egg?*

You kill a chicken for the dinner, gut it. Stuff it tight with herbs, delicious paste. The blood collects and mingles with the feathers. The viscous dribble of the shell-less eggs. Every life is full of possibility, you think. And there are other places you can go.

The ash dulls in the hearth. Waiting to be gathered and scooped out. They let it die right down, and chide you for it. You're a servant now. Only you don't go home to the village at night. You do not sleep in a warm feather-bed beside your husband. You do not kiss your children's faces. You hold your mother's love inside your mind. *Be gentle and be kind and be my daughter.* It hurts you now. A razor and a prayer.

Years pass, and you assume a woman's shape. You are lovely. Your eyes are wide, your skin is smooth and whole. Your limbs are shapely, smaller than they should be, but still pleasing. You like your legs that take you different places. You like your arms that make things, grow things, mend.

The invitation comes to the door with pomp. A footman, short and pigeon-chested, stomps into the hall and proclaims the words. And like a magic spell, the house begins to swirl. Before all this, they lived in stasis. Now you hear the hum of their demands all day and night. Hem this and affix crystals onto that. The furniture gathers webs and dust as everyone turns to work, real work. The kind that turns a woman to a wife. A simple village girl into a princess. You chuckle in your nest at the idea. You run your hands across your mother's silks. Her satins, velvets, lace. The textures and the vivid shades she liked.

He gave her more than he has given them. He loved her more, you think. He loved her more. A small daguerreotype of her kind face, hair a rippling river down her back, is wrapped up tight. A secret in pink leather. You keep it at the bottom of a trunk and only look sometimes. You don't want to remember the stiff formality of someone still. Your mother liked to move. And she was colours. Colours and a voice. And you were loved.

You make candles from stubs of other candles. You like light in your room to look and read. Gillian wants thick, warm, yellow fabric, soft as butter. Lila prefers cold. All icy blues. Their dresses made to measure. No expense spared. And dancing slippers. One night's wear and out the door like ash. You can't even borrow their cast-offs. You wear a pair of boots got from a child. Of sturdy stuff, that keeps the water out and gets you round. Your mother's slippers have little bits of mirror on the toe and they are velvet. She wore that pair the most. You can see the little curve her toes made on the inside. The weight of her. It has a certain power.

Your father is away all of the time now. Even when he's home, he isn't there. At sea, he gains and loses things. Cloth and jewels and spices. Brightly coloured things that tease the eyes. You think about the soft crash, wave on shore. How dangerous the journey out would feel. How wide the possibility. Potential for the lives you could try on. This house, this life, this village. They weigh you down; you're covered up with ash and sunk in tar. You are a thing to comment on. Forget. You are a thing that makes this house a home with two small hands. And they don't think on that, although they should. You brush your hair and braid it round your head. It's not as long as hers, but it is thicker. There's a sheen to it that pleases eyes. People like their women to be lovely. Women are a lot of different things.

Your stepmother's face is very smooth and comely, till she opens up her mouth and screeches like a hawk for you to hasten. You comply. But you are not compliant. Your clever fingers weave a different plan. Rub oils into your aching muscles at the end of days. You'll be a pretty, fragrant thing despite

7

them. You don't care what it takes. You know you'll go. And you will not come back.

You sew the things that you will need in secret, slicing up the little bits of Mam. She was a little smaller round the waist, and you are taller now, but just a touch. The corset fits, but you are done with cages. Kohl around your eyes. The fire dies. You look into the mirror. Eyes that shine. Work harder than you have ever worked and be ignored and still retain your value. Do more than most and smile and be in pain. What breaks a person builds another person. Something strong is growing in your stead. A magpie's nest. Old treasures. A new life.

The day arrives. They skitter round like insects. You brush them off and help them look the part. The sun goes down, and they alight the stairs, their faces painted whiter than their faces. Their breastbones dappled with the pink of strain. They are wearing emeralds and rubies. Ropes of things more lovely than their skin. Vases for their soft pink, plucked bodies. Tentative as deer, they step into the carriage, to the night. You can see the hope etched on their faces, hope and pressure. Not for you. Their world is not for you. Your father loved your mother. But he does not love you. You blink your eyes. They fill with tears. It stings. It melts the kohl. The ash streaks on your face.

You take a horse from the stables. You've gathered enough money for a while. You do not know what's out there. What leaving will mean. But walls are not a home. No matter how familiar their appearance. You need to go. To get out. Need to go. Hair down your back, and gentlewoman's clothes, and a fat black steed with mother's special saddle. Ointment for your muscles. Blankets. Cloak. A fading picture of a sparkling woman. You hold her in your hand and in your heart.

The village lit with candles and with lanterns. You think of market day, parades of cows. And which is best? The juicy meat prepared for royal lips. For royal teeth and gullet. The cheaper cuts can nourish just as well. It all depends on taste. Safe passage in the night, away, away. You sleep inside the forest. Knife in hand, you curl in to the horse. Little things are easy to conceal.

Later, in an inn some leagues away, you look out at the castle. The view through unfamiliar panes is different. The stark shape of it on the distant hill. It's fortified to keep the people safe, and it looks like a prison, thick and grey. The windows little slits for arrows to poke out. It must be dim, you think. It must be awful. Staying in one place. You know the weight. You count the coins secreted on your person. You have enough. Enough to get away. Enough to keep on moving till you find a place that's worth the wait.

Stretching on the bed, with soft bread in your mouth, the taste of butter, you wonder what they're doing at the ball. Who the prince will dance with. The love he'll choose, the girls he will discard. There's nothing gentle in that sort of power. You close your eyes. There is a different world. Where people do things, make things. Carve them out. You breathe the thick, soft air. It smells of hops. You smile and square your shoulders. Sometimes love is something more like rage. It makes you fight. You feel the future, wide and bright around you, kicking in your gut as though a child. The night spreads wide and you have flown, you've flown. The shape of you impressed in attic cloth is all that's left. You wonder how long it will take for them to notice. It is an idle thought. You do not care.

You unclasp the bag that you have taken. Your hands delve deep through metal, paper, cloth. They prise the things you wanted from the others. Pull them, like a turnip, from the earth. And on the feather-bed, you plan your future.

You try on mother's shoes.

The slipper fits.

The Woodcutter's Bride

Outside in the forest, there is deep snow. It brightens the earth and makes this place shine with a false cleanliness that I can hardly stand. I turn my face from the window and concentrate on feeling almost nothing. It has been a pale and honest morning, spent cleaning things and rearranging cushions, distracting myself with pretty, useless touches. Embroidered stars. Some holly in a vase. The wooden floors are cold and getting colder. I do not want to light the fire yet. I do not want to waste the golden wood. It saddens me to think of it so old and strong that turns to ash so easily. We all will, I suppose. My feet are numb and so I pile the smallest twigs and twists of yellowed paper on the grate.

When I was a small girl something happened to me in the forest. I can't recall exactly what it was. It's hard to trust tales from the lips of grandmothers; they come out wrong, too dirty or too clean. Since then I have not felt the same about the forest: I liked it once I think or think I think. It's beautiful but on its inky edges something stirs to fidget with my gut. It's getting dark; my husband will be home soon. I bite down on my lips to make them red.

The bread I made today is warm and soft. It permeates the rooms: a smell to welcome him when he comes back. I must have learnt the recipe by instinct; when first I tried my loaves were nigh inedible: a source of shame and not a source of comfort. But now I find that I enjoy preparing food, for all the act of eating saddens me. It feels so wasteful, something for myself and no-one else, for if I eat it's usually alone. I wish sometimes to be a broad-hipped matron, unassailable and somehow pure. The in-between is what scares me, curvy and delicious. Ripening. Could I protect my bones' delicious marrow then? I can't protect it now; I'm porcelain and hollow, like a bird, or like a china bird with onyx-bright eyes. To have always just alighted on mantelpieces but never flown anywhere, for fear of crumbling. I blink and I prepare a charming house to match my charming figure. *How can someone so small know so much?* he says. *So many woman's things.* He spends inordinate amounts of the evenings studying my face with hands and eyes. What he feels there must content him, he lets go and I release my breath. I wonder what he knows of me. His gaze deciphers codes that may exist alien entirely to me. He reads me like the rings inside a trunk, the scores and notches that he leaves behind. He takes his work home with him, logs and branches. Once-living things that burn, that flake apart.

The crackle of the fire I will set. Its glow upon the soft rope of my hair. He likes to brush it with his left hand's fingers. The other rests in warning on my neck. I light the flame. The tapers and the oil lamps. I know I am wasteful but I need this light so I can tell it's him and not a stranger who will turn the latch and greet me with his voice. The sky pelt-dark. The sky is filled with little glinting teeth.

When I was a small girl I rested my head on my grandmother's lap in the lull of the evenings. I closed my eyes and listened to her speak. Her lap was soft and stale – she smelt of sweat and pine, mixed with the musk peculiar to old women. Sometimes I think I smell it on myself. Her tales were harsh, of twice-born fiends and women made of knives, of wild unfettered things who sup on people, who start at toes and finish up with eyes. I did not think them strange, not at the time, enamoured as I was with the attention, her busy hands removing tangles, lice, and plaiting and unplaiting. The voice that wove. And I was so afraid and so delighted. I wanted more, I wanted her to stop.

The window panes are clear but edged with frost. There are no curtains. It is winter but the trees still wear their leaves. They are lovely to observe, especially when the sun is at its lowest, but underneath their clothes they grip so skeletal, poke and drag at fabric and at skin. It is not easy to be lost in a forest, plump and soft when everything is harsh and grasping out. A forest is lovely

to look at but only to look at. Once inside you can't look any more, everything is muted and in shadow. Supplicants are what the forest likes. The clearest of directions are of no use and once inside this soon becomes apparent. To find your way, you must give in, must root like a pig until the paths unravel, nosing here and there, increasingly perturbed. Desperate, submitting to the tangling and the staining. The only way you learn.

Shallow breaths come quick and mist the glass. My fingers touch the cold and trace a pattern. A leaf, two leaves, suspended without branches. I use my sleeve to wipe those leaves away.

The dark is rough outside and something cries in panic or in fear. It's far away and I try not to listen. The snow is clean and weighs upon the murk. A film of something pure on woods and fells. And when it leaves, it shows things as they are. The weight of that can hurt your eyes. Can burn. It is not a good idea to notice things too much here. Slitted eyes that lead to slitted bellies. Things with plans meander through the woods. Pretty children hide their faces through the paths; they daub themselves with moss. Conceal the smell of soft bread and cheap wine. The gifts they bring. They hide the gifts like shame.

I've never even thought I was with child. My ribs jut out too hungrily, like spikes, they'd not know how to nourish something small and soft and pulsing. He would like a child. Not for itself but for what it would mean. What villagers would say. What a man he is, so strong and potent, that he could make a china doll his vessel. Fill her to the brim with little mewling versions of himself. Small, hungry-fisted men, raging and biting gummily, would be just what he'd want. Not one like me. I'd hate to have a daughter, would scrape her out to red blood upon snow. I rarely bleed, but I would bleed for her sake, and never mind, and never count the drops. And I would wait and chase away the crows. A boy would be too strong to kill. All snout and hunger, he would suckle all my sadness out, and leave me husk-like, motioning weakly, made of ash and breath. My husband's meaty heart would break in two if ever he suspected. Can muscles break, an angry messy breaking? Gobbled up. I would be gobbled up.

I know what I must do to keep safe. Stay on the path, one thing after another. I fill my man a basket full of foods. Swaddle them in tea-towels and brown paper. Bread and ale and cheese and meat and apples. Things that can be eaten in big bites. What a big lunch he eats, this husband of mine, with his axe on his shoulder, he strides the way he munches, into the forest wide and unafraid. He's not yet home but everything is in readiness. He's not yet home but everything is tidy, neat and properly arranged. My mind drifts but my industry never wavers. I don't know what would happen if it did. The fire blazes weakly, nuzzling the grate with half an ashy heart. Still, it will suffice, when he returns cold and hungry. The necessary comforts will await him: dinner, fire, and by it his so good and pretty wife slowly carding brittle wool. These are things my husband likes to see. His proverbs drip with idle hands and rods. He instructs and sometimes he is sad to see my hands so chapped and raw from all my household labours that he clucks his tongue and rubs them soft with butter. He has a rare kindness in him, something seldom seen. I wonder if he's happy. Sky pools darkest blue and night stalks day. Soon I'll hear his hobnails, louder and louder, on the path. Soon, but not so soon as to deter me. There is time yet. Not a surfeit, but still; there is time.

When I was a small girl my granny made me things. Things to eat and sometimes things to wear. I am not a small girl any more, my clever fingers sew and spin and weave. My hands are practised now, they assemble such delicious things. Savouries and sweets. My voice I keep so soothing and so soft. My body lithe, and hairless where there ought to be no hair. Still. When I was a small girl something happened to me in the forest. Good things too had happened before that, but this was something altogether strange and best forgotten. It might not have been what I think it was. Sometimes I would like to be a child again, and other times a woman made of snow.

In a place hollowed beneath the floorboards something lurks. Hidden deep but I have found it. His skilful sausage fingers built this house and kept it, big and ready, but I have cleaned it every single day since his child bride was rescued and brought home. I am privy to its secrets now, can sense its nooks and crannies more than he. I shake out the dread thing he has hidden. Oh, but it is lovely, soft and rough and altogether shameless. It almost smells of skin and bloodied breath. Warmer already, I unlace my shift. Piece by piece I thoroughly disrobe, and hold my treasure up and spread it wide. It soon is wrapped around my face and body. Thus enlaced I close my eyes and listen for a footstep coming close. The edges of my mind are softening. Something is melting. Something is falling down. My heartbeat slows, womb snug and belly safe. I ache for things I know and do not know. Something here is straining, soon it will break and I will feel it break and still do nothing. My face is covered with the safest caul. Membrane meeting membrane, I allow myself to wish for things unspoken. Foreign things that glint beneath the snow and could be filth.

Unremembered colours, rancid tongues that slaver but wash clean. Well-met dangers, safety of a little worried maiden, hurry, hurry. Hoods are funny things. Mostly dark, evoking ex-ecutioners. Eyelids flicker. Wet salt upon fur.

Come Live Here
and be Loved

The little life will tell you what it needs. This small, quick thing
that moves inside, below.

Of you, it isn't yours.

No, not entirely.

You longed for this so hard, you wasted pale. They thought
you'd sicken, die.

Your husband loved you. Childhood sweethearts. Two of
you. Hand in hand, and as the hands grew larger, kisses, rings.
You love him. But there is more love inside you. There are many
chambers in a heart. You've always known his love. You want it
bigger. To leave it, living, after you have gone.

You pray and pray, and still the blood comes from you. A scarlet admonition. Every month.

You hang a hawthorn wreath above your bed, keep hazelnuts and moonstone in your pockets. Pray to God. The moon. The tall stone in the village with a hole through it that pregnant women touch. You rub it till your skin flakes smooth as milk.

You pray and pray. To anything that listens. The lack of child drinks all your joy like milk. It saps and sucks. Your husband worries. You are all he wants. But you want more, you want to give him more than only you. *Come live in me,* you think. *Come live here and be loved. Come take your place. And make me sure of mine.*

You dream of sharp white shapes the night before, and wake up holding something in your stomach. *Little stars,* you think. *She'll be a girl. A boy would be the sun.* A girl is subtle. When your father aged, he said to you, *My girl, my girl, my girl. My sons all left. It's good to have a daughter.* You washed him when he died. Prepared the body. Waited overnight beside the corpse. Kept vigil. Bodies left alone are not safe here. This village is a dangerous sort of place.

Your husband's face afraid when you inform him. A happy sort of fear. To grow a person is no little thing. It isn't like a turnip or a spud. It's not so simple, weaving vein and bone. Your sense of smell wolf-sharp and, oh, the hunger. You ache with it. It gnaws at you, untrammelled through your gut. The pang of it so sharp, like teeth, like fury. A starving ache that cannot be suppressed.

You long so hard your teeth swim in saliva for milk from a specific sort of cow. An Angus, black as coal, with wide dark eyes. The quiet one, who shies away from people and their hands. Who gave birth to the curly calf, last spring. You'd seen it coming out, a twist of hide. So small and thin, no muscle and all spine. The shape of it. The blood upon the grass. It lived an hour. You stroked it, felt a shudder up your bones, your elbow. It shouldn't be. You thought. It shouldn't be. There are human babies too that grow like that. Curled upon themselves. Incapable of movement or of speech. Within the womb, this baby is a mystery. It's swimming like an eel, and you can feel it but you can't control it.

The milk you take is only from that cow. All others are abhorrent. The world is made of things that shouldn't be. And some that should. The balance, though, has shifted. Your husband looks at you. His eyes shine salty. He clucks the meaty muscle of his tongue. He doesn't like what's happening, tries to substitute it, trick you. You can tell. Can taste the red and white inside the fluid. The blood and wrong. You taste the globs of thick disgusting fat. Too meaty, much too meaty. Coats your tongue. You feel it growing full, you feel it bulging. His face afraid, as yours swells fat with blood.

'You scared me,' he says after. 'Both of you.'

You look at him. This child inside your womb is something else. The things it wants and needs. It would kill you if you didn't serve it. You'd wake up, your teeth furred with your tongue, a film of it, the white part scraped all night.

Your child was hungry. It wanted just to eat the things it loved. It loved a radish. It loved that black cow's milk. It loved the insides of your cheeks, just enough pressure to fill your spit with little hints of tin and swallow down. It hated cooked meat. Any kind of poultry was repellant. A smell of egg and you would retch decidedly. A gesture of disgust inside your womb.

You dreamed of little stars inside the black. They rang like bells. And in your sleep, there was a harsh, fresh tang. On the breeze sometimes, you'd almost smell it. Something that you wanted. Had to have.

You munched on mint, and celery. A variety of lettuces. You'd pull them screaming from the earth, eat them down, picking off an errant worm or slug, a little wriggling thing. Intent upon your feast you would dismiss it. He hated to see you thus, who were so delicate. A proper woman. On all fours in the garden like a cow. He didn't understand the life inside you. You couldn't really fathom it yourself.

It needed certain herbs on certain days. You didn't know their names. Not always. And it would send you just a little bile, thick with longing for specific tastes. And you would hunger. Vinegar and lemon. Honeyed water. These are things easily got. But stars. To eat the stars. How could you pluck them out? The sky needs eyes. Everything needs eyes. Like an insect's, God's have many lenses. You pray to Him at night, and tense your shoulders for the little kicks.

Your husband grows things for you. Spinach, mint, butter-head lettuce, soft and yielding. Carrot seedlings flourish in high pots. He seeks out plants with star-shaped leaves. He asks and asks. And people shrug their shoulders. Each night you venture closer to the stars. You dream of cold, and wake up wet with dew. *What were you doing?* You look at your hands. The nail beds dark with moss. Your fingers rub your stomach.

'When the baby comes,' you say, 'we'll love it.'

He says, 'Aye.' His head rests on the top of your head. Where your fontanelle grew hard with age.

Your fingers stroke at your protruding stomach. When you look down, your nails are digging in, like skin was earth.

You wake one night, your fists beating on the wall that separates your house from hers. The smallest fingers of your hands are raw. Dirt and lichen gather in the wounds. You aren't bleeding. Just a little sting. And every mother's told you pain is worth it. You swallow down the fear. The curse of Eve, you think. This is the curse of Eve.

You will not venture in the witch's garden. That place. The toll it takes. The things they say. But two nights later, you wake up, nightgown splayed, one leg cast over. His arms around your waist. He drags you home. And you are raging, starving. It's not your hunger this. What grows inside Something with a brain is living in you. Something with a heart. A little skull. You scream at him. You tell him that it needs things. The life you grow. He holds you and he sighs. His hands are pale with flour. He brushes down his legs and bids you come. 'If visit her we must,' he says, 'we'll go in through the gate and by the door. We'll ask for what you need. It will be fine.'

Fine like weather. Fine like woven cloth.

His eyes are brown. His eyes are brown and kind. The baby's do not have a colour yet. If they have started. Pulsing, viscous bags inside a skull. There is something of the witch about you. Creating life. It almost overwhelms.

You scan your brain for witches you have heard of. Faces change, they die, are born again, but always they have gardens. Hands stained green and nails as short as men's. Skin leathered with the sun, hair unkempt, long curly down their back. Woven into an inexpert plait. Piled atop a head. They rarely leave the garden, but you hear the stories. What they look like. What they do, and are.

If you want to hurt someone, or heal them. Feel something that's died or kill a pang. There are ointments, poultices and words that she can give you. Things that cost you dearly in the end.

The witch has always been there. Has always been the witch. She has three different faces – that your mother told you. One a soft thing, bright with hope. They burned her. Something thinner rose up from the flames. An angry wisp. The town was scared of her, she wandered barefoot, plucking produce from the carts at markets, never asking, taking what she needed. Biting down. They drowned that one eventually, in time. She was fat with something like a child. Getting braver. Getting more afraid. What came out of the water was a terror. Flat-stomached. Bloodshot eyes. Two rows of teeth, and filed to little points. A shark and not a woman. Always moving. Weaving through the crowds, you see her sometimes. Now she doesn't take. All things are offered, bowed heads and low eyes. People only visit her when desperate. This woman-thing. This what-cannot-be-killed.

You go in by the gate. The iron interweaves with creeping plants. Rust flakes among the leaves. You venture in the garden. It is wild.

Walking through the long swish of grass, you feel the baby calm. Someone you have never met is living inside of you. You pulse your hand against the little bulge. The baby is yet young. You're halfway there you think. How can you bear to keep on doing this?

You've never spoken to the witch before. You've never had the call. You do not meet her eyes if she passes. Incline your head to pay her some respect. A woman who has died and come back twice is not a woman. She is something more and something less. Women die so many little deaths. Each time a hope is fisted like a butterfly to powder. Bees on leaves, and little sooty ants.

You brush your fingers over a nearby plant. It bows its leaves as though it could placate you. But you are not the thing that needs to rest. You nudge him and you touch the leaves again. And still it stirs. He smiles at you and tickles at a leaf, so gently it could be a baby's foot-sole. The plant curls to him like a purring cat. *What sort of place is this,* you think, *at all?* The things that live, and suddenly you see it: little star-bells, clustered in the green.

You feel the baby moving in excitement. A sort of jump. *Yes this yes this yes this.* You look at him and point. He nods. He sees it. Then you hear her voice. The rise. A clear glass bell. You thought it would be deeper, less than feminine. You turn. She stands before you, robed in white.

'You venture to my garden.'

She speaks to you. She doesn't speak to him. You nod your head. You flatten your hand on your stomach. See the long cylinder of tower erupting from her house. To the sky as though it were a pencil to a page. You try to meet her gaze. It isn't easy. She looks at you, the deep and searching look that little children give. Before they know it's rude to stare at someone if they know that you are staring. You try to speak. Your voice a little cough. A husky whisper.

'I didn't mean' – you curl your hands over the bulge of womb – 'to trespass.'

She smirks and crooks her head, the way cats do.

'You cannot trespass here. This garden's mine. Nothing ventures in without my knowledge.'

You hold up your two hands; the grazes visible.

'The babe,' you say, 'I want the things it wants. And it is hungry for these little stars.'

She smiles at you.

'Campanula rapunculus. Such a name for such a little thing.'

You lick your lips. Your mouth is full of fluid. Grit your teeth and try to swallow down.

'It isn't me,' you say. 'It isn't me that's hungry. That is starving.'

Your husband stands beside you. He is mute. His eyes are on that woman. On that thing. He cannot help it but you hate him for it.

'What will you give me?' The witch is looking at you. With her eyes. 'For a taste of that which I have grown? Of what is mine.'

You blink. You have no words. You blink again.

Your husband says he has a little gold.

The witch considers.

'May I touch your stomach?' she asks.

You nod. Her white witch fingers splayed. Her dirty nails. Her face is lined and you can see the double set of teeth as white as pearls and very, very sharp.

She sees you looking, asks you if you like them. And you nod.

'Your baby has the same,' she says. 'Or will have. All children do. A small set and a large set, for their adulthood. It's just that these are differently arranged.'

Her wide white smile. Her hair like dirty cloth. Her hands on you. And was this witch a baby like you once? You aren't sure how witches can be got. The seashell nails are scraping at your innards. The witch's hands move back. The same soft motion.

'Hello, little thing.' Her voice is tender. So much softer than a voice should be. There's more to it. A sort of whirr. A croon.

You close your eyes. The life inside you moves towards her. Like the plant under your husband's touch.

She smiles at you.

'The plant that moves is called the Morivivi.'

Did you ask? You cannot recall speaking. You scratch your nose. The sweat is beading on you in this garden. She stands

there moving fingers with your baby for the longest, longest time. It flickers like a fish. It rises, curls. The little stars forgotten. There is an apple tree behind the witch. And it is pitted with a soft white fungus. Something small and dangerous eats away. Your baby squirms with pleasure in your stomach. Your sweat drips still but you are very cold. Fungus is not only for gardens, fields and trees. People can grow fungus too. Upon them. Between their toes or in the mouths of babes. Crevice-welcomed thing, it sneaks. It finds you. Suddenly it's there.

The stranger stirs within you. You blink again. You find your eyes bead too. Your husband's on his knees plucking hungrily at this, at that. The things he wants for you. He fills a basket. You are stuck stock-still. The witch is making cluckings with her tongue. She looks at you and there's a hunger in her eyes that isn't just for gold. Teamed with it a sadness.

'**This babe,**' she says, '**it wasn't meant for you. Your womb is barren. Something's taken root. The seed of it was mine, but it has warped. And I can nurse it back. I can protect it.**'

Your husband stands beside you. His face is blank. He thinks of other things. He isn't here. This bargain must be yours. And yours alone. You are not certain how this makes you feel. Powerful, in a way. Alone in another. How witches feel. Their voices, clever hands. Her eyes on yours. Her pupils needle-points. You feel your moist brow furrow like a field.

'**What you have grown,**' she tells you, '**it could be a danger.**'

'Like you,' you tell her. And your voice is far away. You are under water with this shark. And she is hungry for the thing you've grown. She would cut it out of you to have. And something in your gut says you should let her.

'Eat all you want,' she tells you in that voice. 'Come venture in my garden. But when the baby comes, it will be a girl with golden hair. Like all of us at first.' Her sharp smile twitches. She inclines her head.

'The babe will come. Will eat my plants. Will suckle at my breast. The village will be safe for many years. That's all that I can promise. Walled in stone, this little thing, this girl will be restrained. And her hair will grow long. Will trail the floor. Will coat the walls like tangleweed. Will work at them, erode them. My power and her power. They will clash. But still, I'll treat her with a mother's love. I'll feed her well, as I was fed myself. Oh, little thing, come live here and be loved. Come be a daughter.'

It is the most you've ever heard her human.

'I wanted to …' Your voice is cracked.

She tells you that she knows.

And when your time comes, she will take your womb. It is the way. You only house one thing. When you house this. But wealth will come and illness shun your hearth. There are advantages to growing witches.

She pauses. And she looks at you again.

'**The miller's wife is with another child. They can't afford it. You could offer help. Tell everyone that you have lost a babe. Have money, milk. It will be truth. At least a kind of truth.**'

You swallow down. You smell the small star-flowers on the air. The little bells. Your husband moves again. His ears have opened up, like morning daisies. 'She'll have the baby,' you say. 'We broke into her garden. Stole her plants. The witch will have her baby or my life.' Your voice is sharp. A razor ragging cloth. Hysteria, they call it, when your womb swims wild round your body. Drives you mad. And when the babe scoops out what was inside you, will you then be calm, aligned in humours?

The witch nods. Her voice is like a person's almost, now. '**Aye,**' she says. '**I am a witch, and I can bear no babe. And so I would have yours or kill your wife.**'

Your husband swallows. 'All of this – for that?' he asks, and gestures to the plant. The bells and stars. Calm-something–something-something. The name was long. Your brain cannot recall. You are hungry once again. Once the witch removed her hand from you, it crept in like a dormouse and it bred.

The witch shrugs. '**It is this or lose them both.**' She smiles again. Her teeth look larger. Sharper in her mouth. '**Do what you will.**'

Later, at the table, you munch the greens, the roots. There's a pleasant sharpness to the tang. The small thing stirs. You almost feel it fatten. This dangerous growth. This girl with golden hair. It judders like a tadpole in a stream. Delight, you think. It's squirming with delight.

It sickens you. His head inside his hands. Weighted like a hem with guilt, with shame. You think of the miller's children. They are comely, hearty little things. Sixteen of them she has. And one more coming. Babe to drink your milk and melt your heart. Golden ropes of hair. Two sets of teeth inside you, caged in gums.

God's eyes above, and stars inside your stomach. You stroke the beast until it almost purrs.

You Shall Not Suffer ...

You grew up soft. Your tender heart would nurse a frightened fieldmouse rescued from a trap. Would make a splint. You'd try to help but always it would die. You gave them names. You were a friendless child, a barrel-chested, sturdy little thing who played alone. Who looked up through the branches seeking nests, needing something kinder than a human.

Sometimes dogs lash out when they're in pain. You never minded it, you staunched the wound and then you went on caring. You recognised the feeling in their eyes, the desperate bloodshot bulge, the darting to the corners.

You grew up soft, but still you learned to hide it. Piece by piece. The world's not built for soft and sturdy things. It likes its soft things small and white, defenceless. Princesses in castles.

Maidens waiting for the perfect sword. You grew up soft, and piece by wounded piece you built a carapace around your body. Humans are peculiar little things.

You found a form of leverets abandoned. You tried to take them home. Your father wrung their necks. Five little bodies limp beside the fire. And they were skinned, and they provided soup. That wasn't why he killed them in the first place. He told you that he did it to be kind. The kindest thing, he said, without a mother. How would they survive? Yours had been gone for just over a twelve-month. You wanted so to mother them to health. Their ribs against your teeth. Your stomach hurting as you worked your jaws.

Men don't cook. You had to hold the corpses that he'd skinned. Without their fur, they were a little smaller than your child-sized hands. The baby things that needed to be mothered. You would have done it, could have done it well. A soft-lined box, and old bread soaked in milk. Every little death had taught you something. This one taught you. Hide it. You chopped their meat. Seasoned them with salt. Boiled them to a soup. Made stock from little bones. You sopped the juice with wheaten bread you'd baked. Blood and tears. The taste of blood and tears.

People weave a kindness to their cruelty. Those little lives so salty on the tongue reminded you of that. At night, you folded hardened, ageing bread into your mouth, drank milk to stop the thoughts inside your head from spilling over. The gap in you that needed to be filled was big, was huge. There was not enough bread inside the world to fill the ache. A field of wheat, a herd of lowing cattle couldn't feed you. At night-time you become a ravenous thing. You hunger. How you hunger.

At dinner, you see sauce trickle down your father's bearded chin. The cupboards bare, you've emptied them. Your gluttony is something to conceal. You cannot stop it but you must contain it. This is when the witch in you begins. The small deceits protect you, what you are. Conceal it well from knowledge and from eyes.

You grow up and out, and other girls start to like you more and less at the same time. You are a bulging thing, a lack of threat. Your bulk protecting you from mouths and eyes. Or so they might assume. It doesn't, though, not when you are alone. Men press to you in corners and on lanes. They smile at you and then they move their tongues along their teeth like blades on whet-stone. You see the glint of pink on yellow, white and brown. You want to close your eyes, but it feels dangerous. Your body has become a cut of meat.

You've always wanted love. Or touch. Approval. They sense the need, they sense the gap in you. And they can't name it but they want to fill it. Secretly they want. You do what you are told. You eat at night.

You find a turtle by a pond one day. It isn't well, you need to make it better. You borrow books for favours, read and do. Release it back into the wild it came from. It will be eaten soon, you think. It does not die on your watch. That's a power.

A little section of your secret strength begins that night. You bake a baker's dozen currant buns. Leave one outside. You will not eat them all. You will leave one. A thank you for the gods. You saved a life. They let you save a life. A thing like you, a thing that is for trying and for failing. In bed that night, you gaze down at your hands. Begin to pray.

The bun rests sloppily upon the grass, the morning dew a glaze so soft upon it. You crush it to the cottage wall like clay.

In your bed that night, your mind processing all the things you've been. And all you are. You venture out to feed a lame whelp. He lives behind the barn. He bites your hand. You feed him and you stroke him none the less.

Your father starts to notice missing food. Your bulk a flag, a signal. It increases. People comment on you, like a cow, a dog. A thing. You have become another sort of noun. Although you never felt you were a person. Not with other people in the room. When filtered through a different set of eyes, you pale and flatten. Picture-postcard freak. You rat at flaking skin. Comb your fingers nervous through your hair. As brown as the shell of a hazelnut.

That night inside the kitchen, it appears. A tall and rangy thing. A hare, it seems. But bigger than a wolf. It stares at you. Your fingers reach to stroke its fur. It isn't silky. Doesn't need to be. The job it has to do is something else. You go with it. Your hand upon the warm hump of its spine. It slows its pace. It wants you to be with it. This is new.

You venture to the border of the village. And when you reach the forest, you let go. You have become afraid. What happens there's another sort of thing. It is the place unwanted children go. You've often wondered why you weren't put there. Left to wander, starve inside the dark. Some of them remain, and grow and thrive. They can return, a wild look to their eyes. They work as farmhands, wet-nurses or guards. And when they've gathered payment, they escape. The hare inside the woods. You move away. You don't belong, but you abide here somehow. You bow your head. The glitter of the eyes inside the woods.

You are afraid. But there is something else inside as well. A kind of thrill. You always have been told the things you want. What you are greedy for. The sense of wanting something is quite different. You clean the house, you change the livestock's bedding. Feed the cows and chickens. Living things. A fox has eaten one in the night. Its entrails spread along the dirt. Calligraphy, you think. You place your small hand on the bloody mess. It pulses to the touch. There's something in you now. A kind of strength.

Your father places locks upon the cupboards. Holds the iron keys upon his belt. You have to ask for his permission now. To cook. To eat. You are a woman. Women must be trained.

Your mother was a shadow of a thing. Small dark shoulders hunched inside the room. She would complain sometimes, but not in earshot. She'd hold you close and she would feed you things. Nestlings shriek for sustenance, and oftentimes they get it. She'd rub the soft down of your baby hair. She'd feed you bites. And you would know you mattered.

There are certain things that you remember. The harsh cluck of her tongue. She mended seams. And sometimes he would hit her on the face. So everyone would see he had that power. It happens to you now. It is the way of things. You do not mind. It is the softer tortures that you hate. There is a sense that you have been complicit. Fear stops your mouth; your hands drip cold with sweat, your tongue becomes a swollen helpless thing, blind and tensing, shifting like a mole inside the earth. There is no comfort for you in your body. It is a thing to fill. That must be filled.

The shape of you. A rounded figure eight that roams through markets, aching to be touched. For a kind word. A tender look. Some food. The softer touches are what carve you open. Splayed and red and like that broken hen. They'll eat you up. They'll take you where you roost and ask for seconds. And you'll hate yourself. You'll hate yourself.

The second time it comes, it is a turtle. Wide and flat and round. You think the earth must be a pitted disk like this, a pitted shell for something hotter, softer. Your hand pressed flat to pitted bone, you dip a toe into the forest night. You venture in; it shows you to a clearing. There is a little hut there, specked with stone. A rudimentary thing. The shape of home, but not a proper dwelling. You look at it and love it in the night. The turtle lets you wander, takes you back. It will return. You know it in your heart.

The following night, inside your bed, you feel a harsh pulse just beneath your stomach. You see a flake of skin has lifted off. You tug it like an errant crease in sheets. Your skin comes off as smoothly as a tablecloth. You stand inside the room. You are much smaller. Everything is big. Your eyes are on the two sides of your head. The sideboard and the window all at once. You cannot see the fireplace without turning. Your legs feel fat with speed. You venture to the door. You run. You *run*; your strong legs move like scythes through ripened barley.

The night air hits the furred length of your ears. You hear it all. The low hum of the insects. The lap of water. Rustle of the leaves, the swish of grass. The heartbeats of the cows. You venture to them. Suck your milky fill. You gulp and gulp. They gently let you take your nourishment. You venture back to bed, your stomach full. You are a girl again. But more than what you were. When your skin grows back, there is a little disc between your breasts that's hard as bone, and speckled grey and black. You stroke this part of you that grew last night. It meets your skin so flawlessly, you think. You flick it with a finger. You sense the contact but it doesn't hurt. You were a hare, and now you are a woman. Carapace. You have a carapace.

It is a fieldmouse when it comes again. A fat, resplendent thing, the size of a pony. Its black, beady eyes are kind. You grasp its tail. This time, the branches part for you. Your hair untangled by the rose, the briar. It recognises you, the earth, this place, for what you are. A thing that it should welcome. That is worth it. You venture in, and know you won't come back. Inside the forest you will build a house. Of nourishment. Of healing. You will leave food outside for the unwanted. Loaves and ginger biscuits, milk and cheese. Your body will obey you, warp and change. And you will never ask before you feed.

Years pass. And there are two. The girl's like you. You catch her pulling handfuls from your walls. The currant buns, the gingerbread. The apples. She shoves it in. She doesn't even taste. The boy behind her eating just as hard, but takes a beat to look at her, disgusted. Eating isn't clean. Not when you do it properly. She wipes a dirty sleeve across her mouth. She stains it, doesn't care and keeps on chewing. You like this girl, this little full-of-life. The boy is something else. His face is sullen, cold. He doesn't like her and he hates this place. You run your hands across an owlet with a broken wing. It screeches at you, clicks you with its beak. Does not make contact. You are something else. Inhuman now. You've grown hardness over all your soft, a jointed case somewhere twixt bark and seashell. Makes it easier to clamber in after a night of roaming round for milk. They fear you in the village. And abroad. When they abandon their litters in the woods, for lack of coin or care, they blame the witch in her home of food.

They come to you, in spite of this, to ask for help. You listen when you can. You like to heal. You hear the boy speak harshly to his sister. She chides him back at first. You lick your chops. You grew up soft. But life has grown you appetites, a shell. Your joints click delicate upon the latch. Little children gnawing at your house. You open wide the sugar-candied window, and you call: 'Little children, little ones. Come in. Come in. Come in.'

You offer them good food and a soft bed. You'll try to help but you will not make promises. The things you care for some-times try to hurt. You must protect yourself. And those around you. You welcome in their desperate little selves. Gratitude does battle with disgust. The girl. The boy. You turn the oven on. You get to baking.

Meet the Nameless Thing
and Call it Friend

It was hard for her. A sentence people say a lot. A lot. It's true. It was. It was and it still is. It's hard. It's hard. People think it isn't. When you've money. When you have more than what you had before they think it stops.

It doesn't. The daughter knows that now. From a father to a something to a husband. From big man down to little back to big.

She was a simple thing. Wide face freckled, bovine eyes. More dog than cat. The kind of face that's asking you to love it. The kind of girl who worked to make you glad.

The mother died when she was only little. The mother tall as well, but very thin. A quiet voice, a woman who renounced things. Her little girl, she always took up space. A long, wide baby watching faces come from out of the blur of world. She'd see the eyes and teeth and wait for smile and she would smile them back. Demanding food with little sorry cries. She didn't mean to bother. She just needed. There are things we can't do for ourselves.

Little octopus hands. Pink splayed fingers teasing at the bottle. As she grew they lengthened and they learned. They could do things. Shape and rearrange. Sew buttons, mend tears so close you wouldn't know they'd ripped. You wouldn't call her neat, though, neat or little. There was a heft to her. Not sugar-spun but maybe worked from clay. Mayhap somebody shaped her on a wheel and liked the job so much they kept on shaping. Big lips. Long legs. Sad eyes. And golden strands.

When she grew up, she had her mother's hair. Her father loved it. Carded it like wool, nursed tangles out with care he didn't have for scraped knees, bruised elbows. Always looking for an excuse to touch. Soft pat on the head for fresh-baked bread. Millers and their bread. She'd roll her eyes.

The two of you is rare. Other people in the village had sisters, brothers. Someone else to share the load of work. She couldn't help her father in the mill. He took in local boys. They did the job. He'd take them over sometimes for the dinner. She'd tower over them and give them spuds. Slice flesh and ladle gravy. He'd tell her to 'make an effort'. So she would. She'd take no meat, she'd eat with smaller bites.

One hundred strokes of the brush before bed, and a little oil to make it softly gleam. He'd watch her do it quietly every night.

She'd tell him little things about her day, he wouldn't listen, looking at the gold. He called it gold. Their brains are different, men. At least she thought so. Thought, or maybe hoped.

Straw to gold, he'd mutter. *Straw to gold.* His eyes upon her back. The one good thing about her. Every night. An awkward thing that grew a pretty veil.

Anything that's fibrous can be spun. She worked mainly with wool, bought from a neighbour who kept sheep for meat. She'd wash it in the hard enamel sinks or metal buckets, to take the dirt and lanolin away. The smell of sheep clung still; most of the time it didn't bother her. To know that this was part of something breathing. How dead things out of living creatures grow. The nails. The hair. She'd comb and comb and comb it. Like it was hers. Rough at first to tame, then gentled slow. Focusing on turning fleece to roving. It isn't straw to gold but it is something. Then the work begins.

She knew it well. The calluses on hands that grow from practice. Another thing about her like a man. The size. The want for something more than this. There wasn't anybody that she talked to in the village, not really. Wool and meat and fruit and veg and fields and cloth and weather. Inoffensive things in voices soft. *Hello. How are you. Grand so. Lovely.* And the weather. At Mass, she kept her golden tresses covered with a scarf. Head bowed down, in case they'd think her proud.

She liked to do things. A spindle and a whorl. A spinning wheel. She'd spin and spin and think about her life. The roads that she could take. You take a fibrous mess, and get to work.

The threads and strands, around, around, around. Order. Repetition. Building. Soothing. Soothing.

She'd like a baby. Something small and simple she could love. To love her back. She thought about her husband sometimes. The form that he would take. She couldn't see a face that looked at hers and smiled at her and meant it. But maybe somebody would like her dowry. Like her father's mill, her wide hips, tidy house.

She'd spin before her bed. Fibre into wool. There's so much you can do with wool. Weave, crochet, knit. It can take any shape once you instruct it skilfully with hands. She thought of all the strands while sitting, spinning. The paths to take. The wool itself can't care what way to go, but still some roads are softer than the others. Little seeds and leaves inside the fleece, she'd find. She would pick out. Sheep are more than meat. There's something else to them. That's not for eating. It filled her heart with something, as she worked.

Her father kept on asking about men. Listing names and attributes. Why they weren't good enough for her. His little girl. He looked above, below her face as he addressed her. It was her hair. He loved to see her hair. The rest an accident. His face her face. When he was doing this, she'd clean and squirm. Not good enough just meant they didn't want her but she couldn't say it. It felt too much like failing. He'd lost her mother young. To disappoint again, again, again. What sort of things did he say in the mill? The spin of wheel, the drone of heavy work, the toss of water. His voice above cacophony and strain.

And every night, he watched her brush her hair. She thought of spinning. Something beautiful. She'd pluck each strand from off her aching head and weave it in a scarf to make him happy. But it wouldn't. But it wouldn't do. She saved the strands that fell out in a box. The most important parts of her were drifting off, and she was losing. She was getting lost.

He'd list her good qualities. 'Who wouldn't want you?' he'd say. 'Who wouldn't want you?' It made her stomach weighted down with threat. No-one would and no-one will or did. She wasn't grain to eat, or fire to warm. She wasn't soft threads woven into silk, but thick rough cables pulsing like muscles on the chests of fishermen. Functional. And maybe someone older? Her father wouldn't give her to his friends. He'd keep her first. She'd live inside his house for ever, ever, until the meat of her was thinned to lace. Until her hands grew too warped to clean the dust and he'd be gone and she would be a lonely silent thing then even still.

The whorl weights the spindle. Holds it down. The wheel revolves. The wood is very smooth. She oils it sometimes so it doesn't splinter. The spindle was her mother's. Smaller hands than hers manipulated it before she quickened, grew. A twinkle in their eye. An unspun oily creature. Her father's voice the only thing that lent her grace, finesse. And even then. They both knew he was lying. Speaking of a corpse and not his child.

One evening, she was rubbing cracked hands soft again with butter. He stumbled in. His face was flushed with drink and pale with fright. A piebald, dappled man. She sat him down. 'What is it? You can tell me.' And when he told her, she wished he had not. A man in the tavern, making comments. He'd spoken up, but in his cups the straw to gold had turned to something else. A magic power. Something like a witch. She felt the lick of flame against her boots. Her face drained white as his.

'You need to do it. Need to learn how.' He blinked at her. 'Your mother had a way about her. Something in her blood that called for help. You need to find that love. To save us both.' His fat face gaunt. 'I am a boastful man. And I am stupid. But it will be us both who pay the price.'

She looked at him. He drifted into something then, a waking sleep. He asked her for more ale. She poured it, left him. Went up to her room and slapped her hands against her stupid face that wasn't lovely. She slapped her arms until the blood rose, swelling like a tick who'd glutted long.

The spindle sharp. And could she use that thing to hurt a person? How thick a rope to spin to end a life? How deep a wound? She sat upon the mattress and she stared and stared until her eyes were dark. She set to work. Down to the stable for a bundle of straw, the freshest and the brightest. She cleaned it and she set it out to dry. Best to prepare. In case. In case. In case.

They'd burned a girl two towns over winter before last. For stealing milk. She'd turned into a hare, they said, and suckled long from all her neighbours' cows. A woman to a hare. How would that work? she'd wondered. Did she have to comb her body out into another, fibrous shape and weave herself into another form? Black-tipped ears and smacking lips and teeth.

There are so many creatures in the world. Horrid, grasping things. And was she one? Is the lack she always felt inside her a sign of something broken, something wrong?

Could you unfurl your life? she wondered. Straw or no? Could you spin yourself to something else? The basis for another kind of cloth. Something a little softer, even pretty. She rubbed her hands against her skin and slept. Her father's face inside her dreams was bright. He smiled at her. He took her hand and smiled.

A knock came at the door as morning broke. It was a broad man in an expensive cloak. So neat it was, you couldn't see the stitching. He had to repeat himself, her brain sleep-fogged, her eyes upon the detail of his garb. His voice was thick, authoritative. Firm. He asked to see her father. For a word. She nodded, swallowed. Left him at the door.

Father was slumped, his face pebbled with stubble. Spittle drenched the corners of his mouth. She set to work. She splashed his face with water from the jug. Explained things slowly, and in little words. He spluttered and he smoothed himself and stood. They murmured as she waited in her room. She could hear the low hum of their voices. She knew that they were talking about her. Exchanging goods for services. Gold for gold, and maybe gold for blood.

The harsh step on the stair did not surprise her. The tramp of boots, the creak of wooden door. Her father's face was bright with cheer and panic. He told her if she spun straw into gold the prince would wed her. If she didn't, both of them would hang. His mill and life forfeit. His eyes shone wide. It didn't matter, though. She could do it. She wouldn't kill her ageing father now. She opened her mouth and closed it. Again, again she did that, like a fish. There wasn't air to gasp. She couldn't suck it. Just a vacuum. Just an empty space.

The broad man took her on a journey. Straw and spindle wrapped in velvet cloth, inside a chest. Inside the carriage. Her thoughts raced and her feet tapped and she ratted at her soft and golden hair. She picked at shards of white skin round her nails. Made a little pile inside her lap and gathered it and blew it out the window. She saw disgust upon the broad man's face. She met his eyes and smiled. It wasn't pity.

Hours passed. The castle loomed before them. Spindle-thin, the turrets sharp as pins from out a fat grey cushion. It grasped the sky. It was an angry thing. And what would this prince be, who wanted gold, would marry her to get it? She didn't open up her mouth to ask. She knew from their expressions they despised her. She was just a job they had to do. Another thing upon a daily list of trials and troubles. Soldiers didn't care about the people in the villages, she knew. Protecting those who mattered was their job.

She rubbed her hands. She wished that they were softer. She wished she had her mother's body, face. A pretty woman can take certain risks that she could not. Rough fingers through soft hair. She raised her shoulders, drew herself to her full height and sighed, and followed them into a tunnel.

The room was dark, the walls were stone, hung with large tapestries and tall new candles. She smelled the beeswax and the absence of dust. There were twelve chests of straw beside her. A tray of bread and wine on a low oak table. The air felt almost warm.

The soldier dropped her tools right at her feet and stepped out of the room and locked the door. She ate some bread and drank a little wine. She took her spindle and her spinning wheel from out the velvet. Organised them; then she set to work. Impossible things happen every day, she thought. Why not to her and hers? Why not their turn? The straw was rough, it chipped even her callous-paved fingers, worker's paws.

She couldn't tell how many hours had passed. The straw was spun into tidy little bushels. Shining gold, but nothing gold about them. Not that she'd know what it would feel like, really. There was no basis to compare it to. And maybe straw was gold, she thought. They shared a colour. Why not more than that? Her eyes were tired but she was scared to sleep. She had been left with just a little time.

She looked at the spindle, sharpened little spike atop a spire. Removed the straw and placed her palm atop the point. She pushed down. Pushed down till thick drops came from out her hand and dappled on the floor and mixed with tears. She closed her eyes. The pain would keep her focused. Spindle-sharp and ready for work.

Her father's face. Her father's hateful face. Why would he try to spin her into sorcery when she was only simple, only her? She smeared the hot blood on her palm. She licked it.

And then the nameless thing came out the wall, unfurled itself, and said it was her friend and it would help her. 'What is your name?' she asked it.

'Call me Friend.'

She asked the Friend for help.

'I want to live.' And as she said it, it felt very true. As though she meant it. She didn't know that what it did would work. That Friends appear and they do splendid things, weave wonders overnight, and leave her sleeping there to take the blame. She did not know that its long fingers trailed across the soft nape of her neck as she lay sleeping. She did not know her Friend was always there. Had always been. It waited and it watched. It watched and waited. Did what Friends can do.

'Guess my name,' it told her. 'The one that isn't Friend. And we'll be even.'

'And if I can't?'

'I'll have your first-born child.' It smacked its lips.

She knew it didn't want the child to love it. She knew that it would eat it up like fruit. She recognised the thing. She knew its nature. Looked it in the eye, and called it Friend.

She took the bargain.

She knew, of course, that it would be less simple than it sounded. But for a chance of cloth of gold and silver. The noose removed from round her father's neck. What wouldn't someone do for wealth and safety? For warmth and fond regard. A kiss. A crown.

She didn't know the little moving thing she grew inside her would come out so soon. She didn't know the gush of love she'd feel and then the loss – at the remembered pact. The Friend would come. And it would want her child. And it would have it. She couldn't tell. She couldn't ask another Friend with blood. It wouldn't work. The servants wondered why she turned her face and wouldn't look. Thoughts drifting across straw and searching, searching. The baby cried. Her breasts swelled tight with milk. She called the woodsman.

She only did what anyone would do.

Sister Fair

You are one of three. Your name is Fair. Your father is a king.
And you are lovely. You have two sisters. One is Brown. She
looks as good as you. About the same. Maybe you are prettier.
A touch. The other one's a different story, now. Her name is
Trembling and she is a willow to your oak. A kingfisher to your
finch. A jewel to your darkly polished stone. You do not mind.
They'll keep her in the kitchen. Till you're married. Or they
should do. The way of it with girls.

Simple counting. Ordering. A sequence.

The first one's first. The second one is second. If the third
one married first, they'd know she was the best. They wouldn't
choose you. You are Fair, you tell yourself sometimes inside
your head. Just because she's slender, pale and golden-haired
and special doesn't mean that she's a perfect thing.

She came into the world afraid, afraid. A little baby shaking with the weight. Of all she saw, smelt, heard and tasted. Felt. Trembling is alone with all her thoughts most of the day and that's the way it suits her.

When you were little how you used to try. You'd pass her toys. Tell her she was such a good, good girl. You are the one of them that people like. Brown is hard to take. She speaks her mind and even though she's always polite, the words feel harsher in her mouth to people. You do not understand it. It could be her skin, her hair, her weight.

The weight of Brown is precious. Out of the two, she is the one you'd choose. If there was one.

You washed Trembling when she was just a baby and the little angry gasps of her would flap right up the water in your eyes. She'd scream and scream. And now she's just as quiet as a mouse. Not even as a mouse. She's like a wall. A chair. Not even human. You don't know when something changed inside her. But it has. It makes her hard to like. But easier to take.

The thing is that she's beautiful. You wouldn't know to see her in the house. She hides it, dirt and layers and layers of clothes. She wears the grimmest ones and they don't suit her. Holes and layers of holes. That's all she is. You could lace a ribbon right through Trembling. Might even hold her. Thin she is, and weak. And not like you. You are a different thing to her. It gladdens you but sometimes it can pain you. You are Fair. And you believe in justice. Balance. Truth.

And what's justice but the eldest going first? What's justice but a face being the same as another face? A body just the same as other bodies. Nothing being better, nothing worse. You look at her and think about her value, scrubbed up. That isn't why you keep her dirty, though. She's happiest that way. It has been years. At first you tried. Yourself and Brown both tried. But trying's hard. It's not like giving up. It's something harder. She would scream. You'd scrub her. She would scream. And later she would wince to hear your tread. She is your sister and you do not want that.

You are Fair. Fair-haired and fair of mind. You try to be. You try to look around you. People are the same as you. Just born in different ways. With different parts. You look at them and wonder what love feels like. Is this it? Is this what people say? You've never known for sure, you've only wondered. Trembling knows, you think. She mouths a branch inside the kitchen garden. She likes to lick things. Touch and hold to taste. You wonder who would have her. She's lovely but she's so hard to keep clean. Like smooth white cloth.

Brown looks at you across the table one evening. The fire is blazing. Trembling's on the floor and she is crooning softly to herself the way she does. The little magic spells to keep her calm. 'When we,' says Brown to you, 'when we get married, what will become of her?'

You swallow, nod. 'She will be fine.'

Brown nods, and neither of you means it. Trembling sits behind you by the fire. She doesn't hear things even when in

earshot. You look at her. You want to keep her safe. She shakes her hands and shakes her hands again and then she smiles, gets up and does the dishes. Later, by the fire, she meets your eyes. She stares in them until you look away. That's rare but so is Trembling. There's only one of her. And two of you. You look at your pale hands in the low light. The smell of turf. The slap of wet on flag. Brown is combing out her long dank hair. It seems to absorb moisture in the day, soak it like a sponge, the rain, the mist, or even people's breath. She'll squeeze it out in little nightly puddles. You'll watch them wisp to steam from floor to air.

Everything you gather can be lost. You are you but you don't belong to you.

The first time that you spot him, you know that he is dangerous. Not like a rat that can be trapped and caught. More like a snake, a bright green adder sliding through the grass. You've heard of them in books, sharp, sneaky things. Their bite is poison and they know it too. He looks at you. You smile as blank as Trembling. Eyes to his forehead, in case he would transfix you with a glance. Make you stand there swaying, soft and blank, until he opened wide.

And then he's gone. You know that you will see that man again. And so you do.

Your father calls his daughters to the hall. He's smaller than you remember. Though you were little then. And he's still big. It's just that you can look him in the eye now. If you were of a mind to raise your head.

'Fair,' he says, and you have taken care of your appearance. You wore your nicest dress, the blue and red. You arch your back. You curtsey like they taught you. 'It has been an age. It's been so long.' He looks at you, but only for a second, moving on to Brown, in soft pale green. You oiled her hair and brushed it softly back. It's nicer wild, but folk don't like it that way. They like their women coiled and wrapped and soft.

'Brown,' he says. And something in his eyes is very tender. She curtsies and she takes your father's hand.

And lastly there is Trembling, on the ground. She rubs her hands on it and smiles and smiles. You washed her and you combed her and you dressed her. Pulled in her waist. It really didn't take. She's coming all undone. Something's clinging to her skirts, as brown as mud. She doesn't notice and if she did, she wouldn't mind at all. She puts her two hands on your father's face and laughs and laughs. You realise she really must have missed him. You wonder if you might have done as well. The bright hall and the soft chair and the gold crown and the warm supper. So many things to touch and see and taste. You can't enjoy it, even though you're trying. You're thinking of an adder in the grass. Something small and slick and full of poison. That man had eyes. He had two fiery eyes.

When you were small, your mother gave you Trembling as she screamed. She'd scream and scream. The weight of her would thrash. She hated you to touch. But lay her on a blanket, and don't look, and lie beside her. And suddenly she'd halt and look and move. Lift her little head away from you or close.

When your father stands up, you do not need to turn to see his face. Later in the dark, Brown calls the snake-man handsome. Trembling's humming softly. 'He is, all right,' you say to Brown. 'He is.' But your fingers worry a hole into the knitted blanket, ravelling the strands around, around, until your index finger's swollen purple. Until you hardly feel the thing at all.

Your father takes you riding the next morning. He wants to talk to you. It's you the snake-man wants. You swallow, nod. You knew you would be first. You came out first. It is the way of things. The trees are wild. They grow up straight but all their branches tangle in together. There is no way you can be by yourself. Maybe someone more like Trembling. She'd like to be alone. She couldn't, though. She'd need a lot of help.

He calls to take you walking in the evening. You listen to the hiss beneath his words. You do not like him, but the look of him is something else. The boldness of his legs, his face, his eyes. There's something in him more than worth the hating. At night you turn him over in your mind, smooth him like a cold stone in your pocket, round and round to understand the shape.

You marry someone, then you get a baby and you're safe. You can't have safety, see, without a baby. That's the thing that makes it worth his while. There are other things you can give too. Soft bread and a clean house. Gentle voice, big smile. You wash your body twice that day. Once before, once after. To get the stink of past and future off. He takes your hand and smiles at you. You look at him. You know just what he wants. To bite into your skin, and leave a mark. An apple in reverse. Fair skin around, then brightest red inside and very shiny. You shake your head. You're not the thing he wants, he's moved his gaze. To the softest, gentlest thing there is. 'She likes to be alone,' you say. He makes a sound that's almost like he's listening, but he's not. You think of the long road of your life with something cruel like that. With something hard.

He's over beside Trembling in the soft green grass. There's mud all up her dress. He makes her laugh. She doesn't look at eyes, you think. She doesn't see. You aren't always kind to her. You mock her and give out about her ways. But seeing him, deep pockets and big hands all poised to strike, a thing that's almost love grows in your gut. You close your eyes. You'll try to take him from her. But when they open both of them are gone. She comes home quiet. Hides inside a little corner by the hearth. Her shoes are gone. She has twigs in her hair. She starts when you come close and so you hum. You hum the way she hums, the same low tune. She lets you push your warm flesh to her cold flesh. Shoulder to shoulder, walking dress to shift. You look at her face. She doesn't know the danger of a man. And nor do you, for all you know it's there.

The next day, it is Trembling who rides with your father. He sends her back in a fine dress. She holds her hand open to you. Inside it is a little honey-finger. Crushed around a tiny honey-bird. You peel the two apart and put them on a white plate in the kitchen. Wash down the horse, and hear its breathing slow. 'Did you go fast today?' you ask of Trembling. And Brown is nowhere to be seen at all.

Later in the night, Brown clambers in beside you. 'Why did he not pick me?' she asks. Her face. You love her more than any other person. You think of him uncoiling, rising up. You are the oldest one. And you should have the sleek green back of him. The long legs and strong arms. Trembling cannot help being the loveliest. Being the way she is. And Brown is just as beautiful, if people took the time to look and see. You do not ask her if she even wants him. That is not at all what it's about.

It's not about being sensible, or strong. It's not about being kind. It's not about the soft touch and the kind heart. Beauty and a womb. That's all you are. That's all an adder needs. You do not ask your sister if she loves him. You haven't even asked it of yourself. You stroke Brown's back. You think of both of you as old, old women in this very bed. Dried up together, waiting for a life. And he will hurt her. But you want that hurt.

Trembling smiling less when she comes home now. Father slaps her hands with the flat of his knife when she wisps them through the air. You can tell that things are very loud or very bright or very something for her when she does that. It is a thing she needs to make her safe. He likes her voiceless, and with quiet hands. She hums less to herself. Two eyes. Closed mouth. You see her less, and when you do she's lovelier than ever. Hair coiled artfully and hung with jewels. Soft red dress. The honey-bird and honey-finger rotting. She loves treats but she won't touch those two. In the centre of the smooth oak table, they collect a certain horrid sheen. One morning they are speckled with dark ants.

Things will come to nourish on their sweetness. It won't be you. It won't ever be you.

You are picking flowers by the lake when you encounter him. Nothing special. Dog-violet and sea-kale. Rough clover. You'll bring them home and offer them to Brown and then to Trembling. You'll bake them bread. There are things you can do. He looks you up and down and you feel something in your marrow. You pull yourself up high, and tilt your head. You smile at him. You see that in his eyes he doesn't like it. His arms snatch your elbow, clasp your waist. And you can feel the cold slap of his sword against your leg. Men have weapons. Men have many things. And women learn.

You kiss him on the cheek. You ask him questions about himself. The places that he's been. The ones he's from. 'We'll miss her now,' you say. 'When she goes with you.' The flat palm of his hand against your neck. An adder's kiss. He takes it and you let him. You do not cage his tongue with little teeth.

When you were small, you had a wet-nurse. Like a mother, paid to give you food. She left when Trembling was weaned. Your father blamed her. Something in the milk that curdled Trembling. It can't have come from him, or from the queen. *Look at Fair,* he'd say. *And look at Brown.* The nurse could say that too. Only she didn't. No-one would have heard. She told you a story once, on a crisp lap. About a man who went inside the belly of a whale. And lived there for a while and then got out. You thought it sounded nice. A calm, warm place. The water outside rippling and lashing. You'd find yourself inside the fleshy dark.

You pull him to you and he is surprised. You move in close. His fingers twist your hair and pull a little. You do not mind. You think of Trembling, wincing as you brush. She hates to be touched lightly or at all sometimes. She jumps and she might scratch. And if she scratched at him, what of it then? The water ripples, eddies. Little pulls. The current holds you close inside the river. The weir is vicious and the flowers bright. They say that monsters can take many shapes. And one of them resides inside the river. It's why it foams as though it were a-boil. A thing with eyes and hands that grasps at men and pulls them down and keeps them. It must be that. It can't be lack of strength.

His mouth is still on yours and he is moving his hands across the front of you. Searching for the laces on your dress. The hooks and eyes. The little things you close to keep you modest. When you meet a man, don't meet his eyes. Look down, look down, look down. When you meet a man, you do not see him. You know he is a man and that is all. His fingers on your stomach. His sword belt in the long grass. When adders see their prey, their gaze is fixed. You do not meet his eyes. It doesn't matter. You are a collection of your parts. Fair is beauty. Beauty and a womb. And so is Brown. And Trembling? Less and more and still exactly that.

You think, during and afterwards, of how easily your hands could find his back. Could push him in. Underneath the deep. It moves so wildly, foaming like a cauldron. You are not a witch. You're just a girl. Beauty and a womb. You gather up the flowers.

Hold them to your face and breathe them in. You trail your fingers roughly through the water. Brown adrift and lonely in the bed. Trembling sitting flapping in the corner, face too beautiful for mortal eyes. Your ruined body is awake entirely.

You are one of three.

Your name is Fair.

Ash Pale

When you were little, you were really pretty. People always said you looked like Her. The queen, they meant. Your father called you princess. And that is what you were. He was a king. But everyone has kingdoms where you're from. And it is heavy being white as snow, with rose-red cheeks and hair so dark that combs of ebony get eaten up and fade to naught inside.

You grew up.

Your father remarried. And she was fine and eager, smooth and bland. Closer to your age than his, but that's not a surprise. He's old as trees. As forests. Planets. Worlds.

A cloak. A crown. Will do that to a man.

She was a servant. And that's not important. But it is. The insolence of that for her. The grasp. The thirst. And you had royal blood coursing through your veins on both your sides. You'd always known that staff were not for friendship. Keep your distance. Be a lady. Mind. And then the plump sphere of her little belly. Smug beneath the ermine of her robes. And she was just a vessel. Not a person. Common blood. An adversary's house.

The girl was all the colours of the rainbow. You were four. White. Red. Blue. Black. Those were your ones. She had red and white and pink and purple. Brown and yellow. Green and grey and blue. Most of yours and many of her own. She looked so healthy. Full of sons. Swollen and important little princes.

And you thought to yourself.

Not here.

When you were small, your mother gave you presents. Things to eat She'd made from certain herbs. She had a picture of you in Her head, see. When She was fat with you inside Her room, She'd look out of the tower and She'd think. *These are the colours that my child will be. The shapes she'll take.* And She was always right. You had Her eyes. The shards of winter sky. Of shining ice. She came from other kingdoms, secret places. Beyond the forest, where the women learn of certain tricks. Practices forbidden to their men. Forbidden here to anyone at all.

She held you underneath the water once. Until you almost drowned. You opened wide your eyes. Your pretty rose-red mouth. When you emerged, She asked you if you'd seen and you said, 'Yes.' You haltingly said, 'Yes.' Because you had. And then She held you close.

Your mother loved you. Sometimes taught you lessons.

You blink at the soft warmth of the new wife, muddled with your father like a potion. You lance a boil is what your mother taught you. But she is not a boil. She's something else, more sinister. A tumour. A heavy thing, that's growing fat with threat. And she could whelp again, if it's a daughter. His eyes are up and down her little body. Like it was a painting or a jewel. A thing of value. But she's just a woman. You are more than that.

Have been since you were born.

Your mother died upon an equinox. It was Her time. They choose their own times, women in that kingdom. They sicken and they perish at their will. And She was so much older than your father. She loved you but She wanted it to stop. She asked you if you'd sit with Her. Reciting all the secrets that She'd told you. Over in Her ear, again, again. You held Her hand through longest night till dawn. And when the morning creaked through, She was cold.

They put Her in a box they filled with flowers. To counteract the smell. He said goodbye and kissed Her on the mouth. So did you, and you could feel the stale tang of his breath on Her dead lips. You watched the servants set the box aflame. How things are done. You know how things are done. Your mother told you.

You were really pretty as a child. But as a woman, you are something else. You've never felt desire for a man. For power, yes, but never for a man. You look in mirrors and you fall in love. Your face. Your face. Your mother built that face with prayer and chanting as the birth-pain took Her. She gave you every weapon that She could. And you love it. Your lips a cupid's bow. Your eyes so wide it looks like you're surprised. You never are.

You're eating dinner bite by little bite, so delicate. You do not eat like birds to please their eyes. It's just your way. You like to chew deliberately. Conscious of the life that you consume. Cows have hearts and sheep, you know, like people. Parts of them. Their eyes. Their livers. Lungs. They all have uses. Every part of someone can be used. The world is full of tools, to be discovered. His eyes on hers. You see his eyes on hers and tilt your head. Your voice rings out, so clear, a little bell. Silver fork on glass. A broken chime.

'Father?' you say, and then again, 'Your Majesty?' He doesn't move his head. Not right away. This has to stop. He's not too old to learn.

There is a sort of craft that you know well. Where you can gather things and you can build them. Little shapes you forge at different times. Elemental magicks. Earth and fire, clay-pot blood-sweat shapes. Air and water, tears and bits of hair. And other pieces too. Wood and glass and sand and dust and ash. You do not have to grow them in your womb. They are your servant-children, not your kin.

For you, from you, never ever of you.

Your mother's icy breath. Her dying face.

You give them pieces of you in their bodies. Little chunks. A hank of raven hair. A scarlet drop from what you shed each month. A flake of skin. Your colours. You have given them your colours. That comes first.

And then you give them breath, you give them purpose. Nothing about this witchery is easy. You need to venture further than you have. The things your mother taught you take much work. You have to do it all with your two hands. With pieces of your body, other bodies. Sewing. Warping. Shaping.

It takes work, the hatred that you wield.

When there are seven, you will have enough. When there are seven shapes with life inside.

It takes some months, she's almost fit to pop when you are ready. You wondered if you wouldn't have the time. If you would have another job to do. A little job. You wouldn't want to do that. To force the life out of a royal thing. Once it has left the belly, the canal, then it becomes as royalty. She does too, the thing your father likes. It would be treason then. It would be murder. It wouldn't stop you, but it gives you pause. You close your ice-blue eyes and think about your seven little forms. The different sizes, aspects. You've crafted them. And one by one, they'll wake. When they are needed. When they hear your elemental call.

You sit on flagstones, in the little chapel in the centre of the forest. The ancient one. The one from Gods Before where no-one goes. This place was Hers. A woodland refuge. You mind it well. You clean. You sweep the floor. You sing the blood-songs, offer things on altars. Keep the fires lit and bide your time.

Your voice is sweet, but there is strength within it. You chant the words She taught you loud and long. On Her dying breath, how She exclaimed. Her voice went 'Ahh!' right up and out towards the sky beyond you. You wondered why She did that at the end. What things She saw. What wonders and what terrors. And She was every bit as good as them. Here in your forest home, you grow like Her. You learn about yourself. The place you have. The place that you would take. The shape. The weight.

You've read sometimes of mothers who appear once they have passed. Who care too deeply for their young to leave. You close your eyes. You think about the castle. And it has been so long. Since you got lost. You had to plan things walking in the forest. You had to craft a plan and bide your time.

Women aren't allowed to do this here. To wield the power and to say the words. He'd burn you up, he'd burn you up, your father. Tears would stain his cheeks but he is just. He does the things he has to, like a king. Your mother too. Although She wouldn't cry. She'd know that fire wouldn't be the end. Not for a thing like you. It would take more.

The seven figures lay across the altar. You voiced the things you wanted as you prayed. Sometimes it is important just to ask. To frame the thing in words: *Her baby dead. And all her other babies. Their lives to meat. Her hopes to ash. She needs to know her place.*

You put your fingers halting on the first. You stick a digit in him and he breathes. He doesn't have a face, just little holes for eyes and letting air in. There is no mouth. He doesn't need to speak. You know his thoughts. As any mother would. You slick his face with water and you push him. Out into the world. You wish him well.

The king is looking for his errant daughter. You hear that in the whispers of the leaves. How long it took his lustful eyes to notice. She has blinded him to who he is. The season's passed, the layer of snow is melting. Your skin is white as snow and red as blood. Your eyes are blue as ice. Your hair is black.

Your stepmother is found inside her bath. Full up with dirty water, red as blood. Her face is blank. Her face is white as snow. The child that poured from her is black as coal, a little lump of charred and wizened flesh. An empty leather purse. She lives of course. She needs to live to learn.

When you return, stronger, from the woods, you wear an anguished face, a cape of black, black as your hair. As charcoal. Ravens. Night. Your little sister.

You're welcomed back as though you were the queen and not the princess. As it should be. All as it should be.

Your small thing comes to you as soon as you're alone. You stroke his face and pick him all apart. Little piece by piece. He's clay and fire, you crumble him from balconies for days until he's traceless. Flowers thrive and die where he has spread. You've murdered your first baby. It felt fine.

Each time that you create a little fellow, there's a sort of gift you have to give. A little bit of life. A fingernail. A toe. A smile, a tear. The second one you kiss. He starts awake. This one is made of water and he slides inside the mirror in your room. You tell him to wait there. And in his eyes you watch yourself, your face. There isn't any hardness to your features. You look so soft, a little princess doll. You'd wondered when you thought about it first. If being cruel would give unwanted wrinkles. Would carve a furrow right between the eyes. You needn't have been worried. Know that now.

She's still there. He visits her at night, but she's not glowing. Cold without the glint of life inside. To heat her up. To make her feel important. She looks at him, as though she were a beaten little dog. She knows she needs to sit up. Walk and beg.

You look at her the same way you always did. Perhaps a little kinder. Now that she's disappearing. Not a threat. You can see her folding into herself like crumpled parchment. Changing who she is to please him. Cutting up his meat in little chunks. He pushes her away sometimes now, cuts her off. She has been demoted back to staff.

It's justice you have meted out, you reckon. Sometimes you sit by fountains, looking at the silver ripple face. You're beautiful, you think. But when will things begin to happen? Soon, you hope. You hope it will be soon. You think of your father, calm and cold and made of little stars and wisps of cloud. You think of her, the warm thing in his bed that's pulsing, shrinking. Like a wart that's almost frozen out. The root of her will die. You will be lonely, you realise. When she is gone, you'll miss her little face. A pretty thing to crush. You look around. The bluebirds in the trees. They aren't singing. You are your mother's child. They wouldn't dare.

You smile.

You think of Her. Oak-old. Ash-hard. Blade-thin. The words She said. The way you felt when She approved of you. Or taught you things. How Her big hands would rest upon your brow sometimes at night and you would feel a ripple of bright something, quick as eels beneath the surface of Her skin and know that it was wild and proper power.

You think of them. Small bodies in the centre of the forest. Little things that haven't learned to breathe. They lie in wait until you need protection, might or vengeance. Until you have another job to do.

You think of princesses within their castles. Looking out until a marriage comes. They bind their lives and make their fathers richer.

Not here.

A soft life in a pretty cage with windows. A coffin for a woman while she lives.

And you are fat with sorcery and anger. Things that matter. Things that can be used. You put a bone-white finger in the water. Stir it round, and round and round again. A raven lock falls down. And blood lips smiling. You have drawn a map, and it is different.

Old stories new, you'll venture where you will.

BRINE

Consume
or be Consumed

In the water, things can take their time. Your people traverse the oceans, lakes, the rivers, firths and straits. They mate at sea, but life begins on land. Parents wait in holes that they have dug, to meet their children. The lash of air on face, the weight of bodies that are used to floating. The size of you on earth is something else. Your legs whale-thick, your arms weighed down like rock. You never knew there was a different size to be from what you are. The water you displace with flicking tail. Before it split, it was a royal thing. The weight of it. The strength. And it could take you anywhere but him.

It isn't natural for tails to part like tentacles. There is a simplicity to how it's done. She put her hands upon you. Long

fingers caressing at the soft lace of your fin, and she found purchase. And began to pull. You asked for this. You demanded all
that soon befell.

There is a fish that lives inside the body of the female. She
consumes him and he serves her well. Love takes many shapes.
You see that now. You didn't always think. You didn't know. You
thought a flat, wide back. Smooth skin. And eyes. Kind eyes. You
thought if you were good. If you gave up the things that made
you different. The world you knew. That it would be enough.
But sacrifice is often so invisible. People do not look for it in
others. They know their own. They list them out like titles at a
ball. I've done for you. I've done for you. I've done. And it is
always your turn now. To hurt, to long. To be a broken thing. A
thing that differs. Before, you always thought you were a person.

A soul, they say. The people underneath the waves do not
have souls. They do not go to church. They will know no heaven
when they die. No final judgement. And if you have a soul, the
suffering you do is something pretty. It batters you, like sea-glass,
to a jewel. You hold it to the light and know your worth.

There is a fish that has two little legs and it can live inside or
out of water. It has two arms like you, a splendid tail. It doesn't
need to hurt to venture out. You are the same. But you know
what they think of you, these people. You wanted to be equal.
To hold your head as high as it would go. This little fish. It must
be wet to breathe. You know that feeling.

It hurt, the things she did to make him want you. First
remove the scales. A stone was used. The water kissed your

open, bloody flesh. Then smooth stuff grew, like what you have above the stomach. She pitted you a bumpy little hole. They call it navel. And it means you're human. It is the scar they get when broad hands part them screaming from their dams. They cut the part that joins, then latch to breast. You see things in the palace. The nurses and the mothers. The little humans try to kick their legs but they are swaddled tight, like ocean babies beached. The helpless flop. All they move's their faces, eyes and fat cheeks pulsing, suck, suck, suck. It's similar to certain fish, you think. But there are differences. Human hunger scares you.

There is a fish that lives inside anemones. The poison doesn't touch them. It protects. But others aren't so lucky. The floors here feel as though nematocysts will soon release. As though your death is imminent. The witch assured you that the hurt, while painful, is not actively destroying you. It's parcelled out, the pain she has administered. So much of it would kill you all at once. Her hands upon your tail, your fins, your tongue. She scraped them into several different jars. For future use. The royal blood of a princess of the sea must be worth something.

The palace is made of glass and marble. Hard white things. Bones. You both have those. You see them at the table, left aside. Thin and fine. They mine the sea for food. The fish. The weed. And still, the hungry gather at the walls. They scratch, they shake their bowls. You watch them from the carriage, and you lift your eyes to meet theirs. A woman, old skin leathered by the bright. A scarf around her face, she shakes a bowl. Her legs spread wide. No shoes. No toes upon them. They aren't flat.

And you can see the five small starts of bone. Your prince tells you they do it to themselves. For sympathy. To part you from your money. Your hands flat in your lap. It doesn't work.

There is a fish that can breathe water, air. It burrows deep into the riverbed. It falls asleep inside its mud cocoon. The water dries, and it is left ensheathed. The fish can live this way for several years. Alive and trapped. It lives. It stays. It hopes.

Your toes fan out, long and graceful as the ribcage of a cod, the feather-comb that reaches round the organs. *Do fish have hearts?* a lady asks at dinner once. No-one knows. They smack their lips, move on. There's something brutal in the rip of teeth.

When you were little, Grandmother would tell you vicious tales. Of maidens and of men with roughly muscled arms, speckled with dark or bright fibres. They put the things they weave into the waves. You may not see them, underneath your path. They'll pull you up. They'll take you out and look at you. You'll gasp for water in the harsher light. They'll peer. And you will be ungainly, flapping, flapping. There won't be any purchase for your tail. Nothing to flick you out, away, away. They'll see you with their eyes and they will touch you with their hands. And they will speak to you in guttural sounds, the males pitched low, the females, higher, sharper. Sometimes people go, and they come back. Pieces of them missing, for the men that open flesh to look at. Outside pieces, or behind the eyes. Sometimes they don't speak of what has happened. Or not at all. Voiceless, songless things. Who are they now, who are they? This is why the surfacing must wait. It is not a safe place for a child. It is not a safe place when you're grown. But you must have the chance to witness. Things with legs. And like you. Not like you.

There is a fish that can shock things it needs to leave it be. It uses this for predators and prey. The world is harsh beneath the waves sometimes. Not as harsh, though, as the world above.

The light is sharper here. It strikes you, you are all the time in bright. There isn't any dark. Even in the night-time, they have candles, little lamps that smell of old dead things. Your head hurts with it, more than even feet hurt. And they hurt. She told you that to do this would be pain. You knew, you thought, what hurting was, the weight of it. The depth. But you knew nothing. Here has different rules. Is something else.

You look at him. You look at him and love him. You would be mute you think. Even if your tongue was whole. In your mouth it feels peculiar here. There's nothing to explore the nooks, the crannies. The little bits of food between your teeth must be carved out with sticks. They do that here. Special little sticks to groom their pearls. Your lips are dry. You want to lick your lips and you cannot. You want to speak of him to other girls. They chatter in the night, their little truths, their grievances. Your silence makes you like a treasure chest upon the ocean floor. What's in you won't be found, look as they might.

There is a crab that makes itself a home inside the shells of other creatures. As it grows, it needs a bigger shell.

You rescued him. It was a kind and scientific thing. You wanted to see the shape of him again. Men beneath the water start to peel. Their flesh parts from their bones. It has a beauty but it's not like this. He is a vibrant thing. His blood runs hot. He loves and hates with emphasis. His fingers on your hair. He looks at you. You part your lips and smile. You show your teeth. It means that you are happy here. Above. In the water, everyone just knew. You close your eyes.

There is a fish that swims beneath the sand. It hides itself. If humans step on it, their feet are hurt. You must protect yourself to live near people.

Walking on the beach, and looking out. You could be thirteen again. But in reverse. Your dry head out to oceans, looking, looking. Seeking sisters where there are no sisters. Seeking friendship where there are no friends.

You've lost them all.

You asked the witch for things.

There is a fish that dances with its lover. They synchronise before they can decide how to proceed. This kind of fish will often stay beside the one it finds. Some think it silly but you always liked it. Your people stay together for a time, and then they part. It comes with such a life-span. A year, a hundred years. Hello, goodbye. But you are young right now, and you had never met this kind of love.

You felt his eyes on you upon the beach. The muscle of your tail, your scale and skin and everything about you was alert. They have a story here, inside the castle. Of a princess who once fell asleep. A prince came and he kissed her. Woke her up. Before you rescued him. You didn't know. You'd never been as close to one as that. To one alive. And kicking. How he kicked. Your pretty sailor didn't want to die.

You didn't even know he was a prince until he found you. They wear strange colours here. Like little fish. You placed your hands flat on the meat of him. You pushed and poked and prodded. His eyes were closed but he was not asleep. He wasn't dead. There's something in between. He coughed up water and you sang to him. He blinked at you just like he was a child. The greed that children have for stories, safety.

You thought just then that you could have a power. Something else. That no-one had foretold. You could accomplish something with this man. Sometimes merfolk mate with whales or seals. And that is something vulgar but accepted. With a man. How would you with a man? You wondered. In a sandy bank, you'd lay your eggs and leave them there to hatch. What would the children of two worlds look like? Scaly legs, you think. Shining scaly legs that can do both. Walk and swim and kick and flick and live. You have ten toes. You used to have a tail. You miss it now but you have made your choice.

There is a fish with light-producing organs. It uses them to speak with other fish. To live and love. It still gets eaten.

Everything gets eaten.

The sea-witch is a creature in the dark. She lives inside a cave, deep down, deep down. In the grunting belly of the world. You'd hardly call it ocean. Where she lives. You swam. You swam. Your sisters weren't told. You couldn't shape your mouth to form the words. That tongue you gave up didn't do much good. You'd like it back. You'd like to click and hum to them, untangle their soft hair and promise much.

These things with half of you on pairs of legs. They don't look right. There's something off about it. You often stare. Sometimes you close your eyes. So many of them. So much of this world.

On land, a woman doesn't matter much. You miss it. Or you used to. Your skin is lightly tinged with subtle blue. They think that makes you lady-like. The colour of a person matters here. Who were you once, and what was done to you. They speculate. A quiet thing is often seen as docile. They say their secrets, spew out all their bile as you sit silently beside the window. Staring at the waters, lapping out. Everything is still here, always, always. And it should move. You long for it to move.

But when it does, there is a storm again. They hunt things here. They chase them, not to eat them, but for sport. He likes his meat. He likes to stab things. Shoot things. Have his dogs give chase and bite them hard. That sort of thing makes you a champion. You've eaten fish. You've eaten living things, but killing's always been a sort of trade. You want to live, so you pursue and snatch. You chew and swallow. Sea lettuce. Wakame. Sea-kelp. Little fish, or crabs. The little sucking things that live in shells. There is a bounty, underneath the waves.

Not everything that lives below's a fish. The hum of whales. The click of little shrimp, their fragile legs. The swish of plant. The soft gasp-growth of coral. At home, you burrow underneath the sand. You close your eyes. Your sisters breathing, moving in their sleep. All of you as one. The little movements soft upon your skin. Water displacing. The weight of it. Your limbs feel weighted down and all at once.

Life is that way underneath the sea. You are bigger. And you want life more. And that's a privilege. They call those blessings here. They love their god. He is a tall, thin man who wears a cloth around the parts they hide. He has been cut and stretched. Their god is weak. He doesn't fight it and he just accepts it. They call that holy here. A passive thing.

There is a fish that isn't quite a fish.

You visit your prince in his rooms at night. He looks at you. You rub your head against his neck. You try to make a sound. It doesn't carry. He walks you to your chamber. He doesn't want you. He thinks that you are something weak and soft. Something he could take advantage of. Akin to a small child. It could amuse you, if you hadn't worked for this. You had to hold your jaw wide open as she cut. The water misted with blood, until her features blurred into each other. You are not a thing that sits and waits. You try again. And that makes you a whore.

There is a miracle they talk of here, with fish. It is to do with feeding hungry people. Half of you was once for eating here. Women are consumed in other ways. He will not have you and it's killing you. Crying salt into your soft, clean sheets. Your tears don't smell like theirs. The salt is different and they smell like home. All of you is meat here. Woman, fish. It's all to be consumed. That is your purpose. They cover up their breasts with layers of clothing. It confines you. Itchy. Heavy. Wrong. Your skirts float all around you as you dance. You think of jelly-fish. Their tentacles, their bodies. In these clothes, your shape is quite like that. Without a sting.

The boat upon the waves is very large. It's painted merrily. Gold and red and white. The gaudy brights they like. He's with his bride. And they are going to visit her father. In another kingdom. Far away. It could have been your story. It is hers. She found him on the beach after you left. And he has found her back. And they are married.

She is beautiful. She carries herself quietly. Her hair is the same colour as her skin. They call that blond. They prize that colour here.

You are being given as a prize. Her father loves the pretty women. Dancing. And when you dance, your feet ache. Glass and knives are sawing them in twain. It's the split all over again. The carving that she did. To you. In you. There are things that witches do to women, if they ask them. Your sacrifice. Your power. You thought that they would look at you and know. Your eyes the same. Your chin. Your regal bearing. You did not think that you would have to dance for him to look. And yet you did and still it made no difference.

An animal, you are. A wild, dumb thing, but still with certain talents. A pretty little flower in a bowl. And he will watch you pulse, and he will feed you. He will give you shelter. Stroke your hair. And you will bite down on your lip. You'll look at him and think of your jaw releasing, your teeth extending to meet his.

Of expelling ink to cloud his vision. Of hurt and of escape. They are just thoughts. You are a soft thing now.

There is a girl who wants to be a fish again. She didn't know what land was like before. She'd only really seen it from the outside. An exotic place. A different thing. And it is lonely here. This girl is lonely. Lonely with her legs, her stump of tongue. Her aching legs and feet. Her broken heart.

He thinks you are a thing that you can give. A gift. You see his wife. She is a person. You don't like her, but she is a person. Her throat makes noises and he strokes her hair. His eyes upon the curve of her spine. His fingers on the soft skin at her collar.

There are fish that like the taste of men. It doesn't happen often. But it happens.

You are stuck here. You don't know what to do. The sea-witch told you, you would earn a soul if you stayed here. If he could love you back. You didn't know what a soul was, at first. People speak of them here, as though they are a promise. And if you sin, the promise crushed inside the fist of God. And you will burn for ever. Their skinny god sends people down to roast, if they do wrong. You imagine the indolent wave of those long white fingers.

You run your hands across the smooth side of the boat. The polished wood. You hear the beat of water like a heart. And then a sound. A head. A shoal of heads. Your sisters' faces. You begin to cry. You're making sounds. You didn't know you could. Their hair is gone. They gave it to the witch. They want you home. They want you to come home.

You look at them. You do not say a word. You take the knife. He's sleeping in his cabin. She's there too. You pull the blanket off so tenderly. As though you were a lover, joining in. You do not want her woken. You plane your hand against his white stomach. The hair on it is sparse. His ribcage rises, and his skin is warm. You tilt your head and concentrate. You feel it now. The movement of a heart. And yours is jumping up inside your throat. You close your eyes.

You are not a gift. You're not a thing. You slide the cold blade in. He doesn't struggle. There's a certain witchery to this. You feel the ache inside your legs abate. And it is time to run. Your two feet hitting planks of splintered wood, you leave your clothing littered like old shells, up the stairs and out upon the deck. They see you, and their faces.

And their shining faces.

You are a precious thing.

You're going home.

Doing Well

Frogs grow from spawn. Transform into tadpoles. They have spiral guts, and they are soft. Frogspawn must be protected. Do not remove it from the lake or pool. Observe the miracle of nature's changes. They are your prince's kin. Respect that link.

In every castle there are hidden rooms.
For hidden women.

This frog of noble birth was once a tadpole. Confined inside dark waters by a foe.

In the chapel, candles have been lit to Fertility, Obedience. Their faces sweet, they stare out from the plaster on the walls.

Fertility is wide, her mouth a wound. Obedience is pale with want, with thirst. Too good to ask for what she really wants. Fertility holds a well-shaped sheaf of corn in her fist. There is a baby sucking at her breast. Obedience looks down, her mouth a slit. Thin lips, big ears. There is no need to speak. The candles blaze. The murmured lull of prayer.

Stout body. Protruding eyes. You have heard stories. About what is coming. Cleft tongue. Limbs folded neatly underneath. Skin a pebbled, puckered dirty green upon the back. And on the stomach, pink and smooth as babies. But translucent. You can feel the thrum. Its little heart. When he's on top of you, you're told you'll feel it.

Take my burden.
Give me strength to bear it.
Keep me good.
Please keep me sweet and good.
I would be good.
(Repeat as necessary)

An amphibian can move on land, in water. Can survive inside a mix of both. Certain species exhibit a preference.

You sleep in the chapel the night before the ritual. Anoint your face with seven pungent oils. You put your hands into the holy water. A little gurgle as you pull them out. You are not ready. There are skills you need and do not have. There is no time.

You are to address him by his proper title. Not to meet his eyes till he moves first. He may reach out his sticky tongue to taste your skin. Do not flinch from this. You are his bride.

Your hair is washed and dried.
Water for purity.
Air for clarity.
Your face is smeared with brightly coloured clay.
Earth for fertility.
Your eyebrows singed to darken on your brow.
Fire for protection.

A witch can put her hands upon a man. And change him. It takes a witch to change a princeling back. Cold to warm. To bring about a change. To save a kingdom.

You have been marked from birth for just this purpose. Cloistered with the others. Secret spaces deep within this place where girls are trained. But there are passageways to keep you safe. You've only seen a few men in your lifetime. You are hidden. Not their rose to pluck.

They know you're his. But men can still be tempted. You need to hide to keep your body safe. The body that is his, or will be one day. And you have always known the road ahead. Every year, another babe is chosen. Nobility and peasantry alike. It varies, according to the seers.

His skin is glandular. It may secrete royal mucus upon yours. To brush this off is insult. Do not touch it, and if you must, keep smiling as you do. As if it's gold.

Always a girl. Always lusty, cross. An unsettled, hungry little yoke could be a witchling.

He may address you in his cracked frog voice. He can produce a range of different tones. And you must listen.

You do not remember who your parents are. Witches come from everyone and no-one. You were raised inside the castle walls. With certain skills. They like their women delicate, these princes. He will turn his hobbled little back on you if you don't meet his standards.

He has grown an extra leg. Do not look directly at it. Do not refer in any way to the extra leg. By no means refer to it as a tail. It is not a tail. It is an extra leg.

The little chain, with padlock, is applied while you are still a babe. After they choose. Links added every year around your neck, as you grow. And if you grow too fast, or thick, then it will start to eat into your skin. Will strangle at your windpipe. Every breath a battle. Every beat. Your fingers trace the shapely weight of it. And what will it feel like, to be without one?

His fingers, toes are webbed. And you will kneel while he works at the lock. This could take hours. Do not make a sound. Your prince will open you. And you must let him.

The orb is beautiful, inlaid with arcane symbols, lapis lazuli, mother-of-pearl. If you submerge it, let it fall and drop, his moist grey hands will grasp it through the water. He'll break the surface holding it towards you. Close to your skin and his, it will burst open like a bud, and you will reach your fingers deep inside the golden core. There you will find a key. You'll pass it to him, and then he will unlock the chain around your neck. Begin the marriage.

He may camouflage his skin to match your dress. This is not a good sign. It means that he feels threatened by you. This will end the process – and your life.

The smell of incense and the chanting low. Rhythmic. You breathe it in. It's said to fog the brain.

When he eats at your plate, you must eat with him. You must put things he has touched inside your mouth. They will taste of him. You must not wince, or acknowledge anything but delectation.

The king's beardless, clean-shaven for the occasion. The grey hairs at his temples kiss his crown. Your eyes are low. You walk towards him, thinking. You need to be as sharp. A needle-knife. His hands are large and wrinkled, lightly haired. You feel the meat of them upon your own. Head lowered. Breath held in.

When he sips from your bowl, you are to take a deep draught imme-diately after. If he approaches you after this, it is a sign. You are to stroke a finger down his back. Remember, on no account are you to wipe it afterwards.

You take the orb.

And you approach the well.

He may clamber upon your lap. This will leave a stain that's shaped like he is. You are to smile, to listen to him. Your body may begin to respond with panic. Force this far away, and if you cannot quell it all entirely, pretend arousal. This will be believed. He is a prince.

The cleric recites the story of the witch. The one who cursed His Highness. Her crimes, the punishment she underwent.

In the night, he will clamber into bed with you. His body will crawl over yours. Do not encourage or discourage this. You are for him. And this is perhaps how the spell can be broken.

You drop it in. The cold plop of the orb against the water.

You may excrete a spawn when time has passed. A clutch of golden orbs. It is not for you to know their purpose. If he doesn't change, then you are just a girl. You will be free, to live inside the cloister with the rest. Their hands and voices have prepared you well.

You kneel. You close your eyes. You kneel and wait. For it to clamber up.

The Prince.

The Thing.

Your husband.

But if he does, if the shape he once had rises in him. Then, my child, of course, you are a witch. And you shall burn.

The Tender Weight

We are made of bright stuff and of water. There are several chambers in the heart. Space in fleshy rooms for blood and secrets. Wives and husbands. Tender pains and sharp ones. Love and loss.

And love. And loss.

And loss.

You marry him as soon as you are able, a sennight after the first blood-curse arrives. You are the third girl, least fair of face and quietest by nature. Your corset digs into your gut as you walk down the aisle and take his hand. Your father wraps a gaudy scarlet ribbon about your wrists and his. Around, around. It's looped as tight as braided coils of beard. The red. The blue.

It is the brightest thing you've ever worn.

You'd heard of him, of Bluebeard, before you were betrothed. Of course you had, he has had wives before, so many wives. His promised hand may lead you to your death. You look at the smooth skin on his face. Unweathered pores. He looks so young to be an old, old man, you think. He looks too smooth to have had so many wives. But people say he has. It must be true.

You close your eyes. Believe what you are told. His hands are very firm upon your own. The warmth from them as you are bound together. Stranger. Daughter. Man. Beside, atop you. They hang the bloody sheet outside the castle walls the morning after. The contract binding. There's no going back. His hand on the small of your back, guiding you towards his carriage. The blue veins of your skin pulse strange with blood.

He smiles at you often, his teeth bright chunks of marble in a mouth. They are so pale, they make his skin look darker. Night sky and the moon. His beard is blue. You want to touch it, but you do not know him. You do not know this man. And you are his.

The first night, your nails dug little crescent moons into your palms. His mouth upon your body and his hands. Your eyes shut tight. You do not show you hate it or you like it. You are not sure. You only know it's new.

Your mother's voice winds through you on the road. A list of rules to guard you. Keep you safe. *Be moderate in all things. Wait, and look upon your husband's face and then react. Allow a short pause. It is better to be thought a little slow than to upset your husband.*

It isn't hard to be a little slow. The world is fast, surprising. Unsurprising. You live within it and you must relent. Swim with the current lest it pulls you down. You feel the layer of road beneath your seat. The dust, the stone. Your tender skin can feel them through the leather. Princesses are bred to feel things more. To fear the ways in which the world can hurt them. To close their eyes. To listen. To say yes. To bruise. Your fingers trace the curlicues and vessels on your skirts. Around, around, and under. Interlinked.

Her fingers on your shoulders, pressing, stroking. Her hands winding through your hair, unsnagging knots. Your mother is gentle and definite in all things. She is the only other one who has touched you with affection. It is a strange sensation. His hand on yours. His eyes upon your face.

He is a man.

Your strange new home is far from where you've spent your life until now. There are lakes and rivers in between. Vast swathes of land cut into little shawls. Your family, your father, mother, siblings distant. It would take days for them to make the trip.

You have six brothers and five sisters. Your mother is a good, productive wife. You need to take the herbs that she has given you. You need to hold your legs up in the air. To move them as directed once he's finished. Little tricks to help you to conceive. Each baby is a link upon a chain. Securing you to safety in his world. Vows can break and ribbons be untied.

He has had wives before, this husband who is looking at you now with such soft eyes. You have heard the mystery of them. The missing women. No-one knows exactly where they've gone. And you don't dare to ask. The soft lull of the carriage underneath you. The rustle of your skirts. They sound like leaves.

Your husband's voice is weaving words like spells. This man– who is he? He tells you of his castle by the lake. And on the highest tower, you can watch the sun rise on the surface, and the set of it upon the hills. If you look across the mirror water, you can almost see your father's house. The dark jut of the fortress on the mountain, small as a tick, and just as full of blood. He offers you a bunch of metal keys. 'They are for you,' he says. 'To use. Except for this one. If you find this door, please do not look. Or come and find me, Wife, before you do.'

His voice is low. His face is hard to read.

You are his wife.

Your mother was your father's seventh marriage. The others didn't work. Their insides shrivelled up with time and woe. There are some wombs that cannot carry children, not to term. And if that happens, you can break the contract several ways. You can send them back to their fathers, or you can have them given to a convent. Or killed. Killing is the swiftest way to do it. The nuns and fathers ask for money first.

You think about your future with an empty womb. A world of women, or the home you know. You are not sure that he would have you back now. Blood on the sheets, your value has decreased. Something closed within you has been opened.

There is a thing you didn't know was there, and here it is. You fight it in the night, the urge to reach your hand to touch his back. To smell him like a bitch would smell her pups. There is a little animal in you. It flutters when he asks permission, waits. You answer him. You do not meet his eyes unless you must.

At home, you were so tired, always tired. There are so many things that make us who we are. And your fatigue was one. Loss and lacking on you like a weight. You wanted simply to remain indoors. To be confined. Kept out of sight. If you could shrink. If you could be a little, little thing it would be easy. Creep around the house, as dusty as a moth and as unnoticed. But even little coins are there to spend. They lifted up the rug, and there you were.

You are tired here, but something in your brain is busy, woken. Acclimatising. Learning to survive. One evening, after dinner, he asks you to accompany him on a walk. You go into the forest with your husband. The moon is bright outside when you return. You have heard the screams of chatting foxes, the click of owls. 'There are always eyes upon us,' your husband tells you. 'Everywhere we venture, there are eyes.' His thumb upon dark circles under yours. You look at him. You flick your eyes right up to drink him in.

You start to choose your dresses in the mornings. Curl your hands through layers of cotton, silk. What would your skin like to feel today? What colour would you look at on your lap? He curls small beside you in the bed. You become used to warmth in the night. You wake one morning with your foot pressed close to his. It doesn't feel like duty or a threat. It feels like something else. You do not have the word for what it is. Witchery, perhaps. A sort of spell.

Walks and speaking can't help but continue. You spend time in the library, with the books. You can put your hands on all of them, the small ones and the big, the leather-bound. They are all for reading. You like to see the pages that have marks, or little notes. You begin to learn the shape of Bluebeard's castle. The bustle of the kitchens, the cool shade of the lilac sitting room. The chambers here in different styles. You count them, and you think about his wives. Who came before.

You do not like the thought of them, these women who have known him. Who have had him. Their traces left, a dusty mandolin and some sheet music. Embroidery half-finished in a basket. Red hair upon a brush, the smell of tea-rose on a writing set inside a desk. They are a collection of pretty, subtle things.

You eye yourself in the mirror. Your face, your body, eyes. You are moderate, approaching ugly. There is no art to how your form is shaped. You do not have the finest taste or wit. You never craved approval or men's eyes. You haven't cultivated little tricks. A laugh like silver-bells, or scented hands. He never mentions them, the other women. You wish that you could raise your voice to ask.

You don't know what he'd do. Your father's hands across your mother's face, around her throat. There are ways that ladies can be trained behind closed doors. To do, or not to do. You do not want to be in need of lessons. You do not want to start to fear his hands. You take a horse around the castle. Look at the walls. How thick and strong they are. It would be hard to leave a place like this one. It would be very hard to go back home. Your hands upon the low curve of your belly. You bled again today. You need to work.

You have the servants prepare another chamber, but he visits it to ask you why. You tell him haltingly, using metaphors. Gardens, blossoms, walls. He looks at you. He tells you that he is used to seeing blood. And he would like your company this night. He does not leave the room immediately. You begin to gather your things, to follow him. His hand upon your elbow.

'I would like your company,' he says again. 'I do not demand it. If you would rather sleep alone, then …'

He pauses and he gestures to the bed. His cheeks look very pink against his beard. You smile at him. You realise he's blushing. You smile again. His face is like a book you've learned to read. And there's a rush in that. A warmth. A power. You take your hand and touch it to his cheek. Your husband smiles.

You comb your hair before you go to sleep, and braid it tight. Your husband stays your hand. He takes the braid, unravels it. Begins again. Loops a ribbon neatly. Your braid curls softly down one shoulder, fat and thin bits looping in together. It is the same arrangement as his beard. He asks you if you like it, and you do. You smile at his reflection in the mirror. His two eyes crinkle back, as warm as his body in the bed.

There are choices that a person makes. You feel yourself choosing to like this man. Your hand flat on the warmth of his sleeping back. There's so much blood in him, you think. Compared to you. Your skin is cool as marble. You have always been a little cold. Your hands on your own flesh. It's not as pleasant. There isn't any comfort in yourself.

You begin to properly explore. Taking one room after another, working your way up from down below. The cellars full of wine and the old dungeon. There aren't any chains there. In your father's house, he uses chains. The walls are clean and empty. There are wrought-iron doors, but they're unlocked. You venture in, and sit upon a low-down wooden slat. The door is shut. There is a little hole in the middle. You don't feel any different. It's the same. You stand up, smooth wrinkles from your skirts. And you continue. Key by key by key. You rarely find a locked door in this castle. Sometimes you think you do, but there's a trick. A way of leaning on the handle, quirking at the knob that clicks it open. The keys together, useless round your waist.

He asks you, 'What have you been doing, Wife?' at dinner, and you tell him. He asks you what you saw. You tell him about sitting in the dungeon. About the soft calm of the wine cellar. The rough floor of the kitchen. The good smells. He tells you that you seem to like it here. It is true. You do. You smile at him.

Next time you venture through the castle rooms, he accompanies you. He tells you stories. Of this person and that. Visitors he's had and what they've brought and liked and eaten, said and noticed. You see the rooms through people's compound eyes. He has made a sort of insect of you. Seeing things with many different lenses all at once.

In certain rooms he talks about his wives. Their names. Persephone. Hydrangea, many others. Celia and Mary. Winter. Beth. He uses the past tense to talk about them. You notice it, and every time it lodges like a bone inside your throat.

His eyes on theirs. His crinkle smile. The heat of him upon them. You are not a thing that people want. Or are not used to being so, at least. You're glad he wants you. Speaks to you about things. You feel the questions rising up like bile inside your gut, and swallow down. Your father's face. His hands upon his belt. It's better not to ask things or to want things. Your heart is asking and your body wants.

As you ascend the stairs, you notice that these tours are getting longer. You are using up the metal keys, investigating cupboards. Learning little things about this man. You ask him once what happened to a wife he mentions fondly. His eyes are sad. He says he isn't sure. He hopes that she is somewhere better now. And you believe him, but don't understand him.

That night he sleeps, and you stare at the canopy above the bed. The embroidery in candle-light looks dark as black-work. You know that there are colours in the day. But shadows gather and your thoughts collide. What happened to his wives, and will it be the same way, then, with you? You are not half as good as other women, and you know this. You have always known. Your hair, your teeth, your face. When you first bled, your father came, examined you. You stood before him, shaking in your shift. He walked around. He pointed out your flaws. They wrote them down.

Legs hairy.

Face afraid.

Nose beaked, and with a septum oddly shaped.

Teeth small.

Lips chapped.

Skin pocked.

Thighs mottled (silver marks).

Stomach disproportionate.

Navel grotesque.

Buttocks asymmetrical, and breasts.

He did not ask how you were at your lessons. You knew that you were just a thing to sell. Advisors wrote it down inside a notebook. Your clothing was adjusted to conceal the flaws that clothing could. Your shoulders heavy and your stomach empty. You couldn't eat that night, you couldn't eat.

When he puts his hands on you, as though you were a precious thing, you wait for him to open up his eyes. You think about his other wives, their hair and scent. You wonder who they were and what they looked like. And, oh, you hate them. For being more, when you are so much less.

The castle has been exhausted by you both, and yet the final key has not found a home. He doesn't mention it, and you don't either. And still you spend the time. You walk together and you speak or do not speak. You think less of his wives, and more of your future. You would like, you think, to learn how to run a house such as this. You have watched the housekeeper, the maids. You have a few ideas. You ask him, and he looks at you and nods. You start to learn, and find it satisfies you. To quietly arrange things to your taste. You do not want a suite of rooms, a portrait and a colour. You want a sprig of lavender in every linen closet. You burn sage in the bedchamber. Protect what's yours. This castle is your place now. You have carved it out. It's taken time.

The keys upon your belt. Against your hip. You could lock him in or lock him out. Just as you like. You braid his beard in the mornings, your hands weaving through the cobalt sting of blue. The fibres warm and springy to the touch. It takes a little while to get the hang. You've never had a beard. You didn't know. He looks less and less like a pirate, and more and more a friend. A comfort that you have inside your life. Your face between his shoulder blades, your hips against his legs. You have him, and you hold him as you drift.

Time passes.

Days and months.

And even years.

It is dark when he wakes you. The flash of him, he slithers out the bed and dresses in a trice. You pull a robe around yourself. He tugs your hand. His face is someone you have never met. An old, sad stranger. But you love this man. He tells you it is time. You don't know what he means. You do not understand. He looks at you. He shows you, in his palm, a tiny key. You take it in your hand, and he pulls you up a little spiral staircase, and another. Almost up until the very top. There is a little door. He passes you the key. It is earring-sized and very cold. His breath is panting and his voice is soft.

'You need to open it, my love. I'm sorry.'

You open it, expecting, you don't know. Broken wives have vanished long before this; you know the sort of man your husband is. The spell he casts. The way he makes you brave. There are questions you have asked and haven't. You have allowed yourself to become soothed. You crawl into a little passageway, and he is there behind you, folded over. As the passage widens, you realise your hands are wet. You rub them on your skirts but you can feel the stain that's left behind.

And then he lights the candles, one by one. They line the chamber. Deep and dark. And bloody. It's a gaping chasm stretching out.

And one by one, you start to see the bodies, out on racks, slumped over on chairs, hanging from thick nooses on thick frames, six, seven bodies deep, they hang like grapes together, dark and vacant.

'What is this?' you ask him. 'What is this?'

You see they have his eyes. His nose. His face.

He looks at you. His face is very calm and very sad.

'I had hoped you'd never have to see.'

You tell him, 'Tell me.'

And one by one he walks you through the deaths that he has died by human hands. 'My mother was a witch. And I have witch blood. I keep on coming back. I don't know why. It isn't right. There's something wrong with me. I keep on dying but I can't be dead.'

The first time that it happened, he was married to another girl. They were young. And they were very happy. Her father came to settle a dispute over some land. They fought, and he was hit, and fell unconscious. He woke up in the room beside a corpse. And when he looked, he recognised his features. It was him. The body there was his, eyes open, one deep wound, a cave inside his head.

The second time was poison. He woke up here, corpse foaming at the mouth like angry tide. The third was hanging. Several people joined in. The fourth was fire. Fifth was blades again, but in the back. They chopped his head off, sixth time and the seventh. The eighth was drowning, head held in a barrel until he flapped and popped and gasped his last.

The ninth one took a while. He calls it torture.

You stop his mouth before he tells the tenth. You can't take more. The pain of it. The hurt. The chamber burdened with so many bodies. Piled sky-high, like wood upon the fire. Again, again. He's died. He's dead again. Your heart has stopped, but it is swelling, swelling. Fat with grief and fit to burst apart.

And how is it you've come to love a corpse? A gang of corpses? But he's a man. Your husband is a man. You can't explain.

'Unburied,' you say, as you think it. He tells you that he tried. He tried and tried. He just kept coming back. He always came back here. Inside this room. Fresh and wet with blood. He stopped. He didn't know what else to do. He would wake, would lock the room behind him. He would live. And he would find a wife. And they would come. Always a different hand, a different death. Sometimes, he says, the methods overlap, but there are flavours. Harder. Softer. Slow.

'Your wives?' you ask.

'My wives became my widows. They left the castle when they saw me die. No call to stay.'

'And they …' You move your hand around the room, around the stacks of different husband-bodies '… are you.'

He looks at you. His eyes. His vacant eyes.

'Yes,' he says. 'Each one of them is me. A different love. And then, a different death.'

You know your husband means a different murder. You hadn't thought. You hadn't known to look. The wives. The lack of children. You had assumed the danger lurked inside. Your father's hands around your mother's neck. The squeezing. Squeezing. People in the room who looked away. A heavy ermine collar at her throat. The purple finger marks so livid clear. You close your eyes. You are too full of everything and nothing. You cannot cry. You stand there, looking, looking. You take it in with swollen, broken eyes.

His mother was a witch. And there is something magic in this man. He is worth keeping.

'Do you remember things when you come back?' you ask. Your husband nods his head. You keep that safe. But there's a hurried frenzy to his gait. His fingers on your spine direct you on, through the cavern of the room, until you reach another door entirely. He did not come to dwell on different deaths. Blood on the floor, and blood upon the dark hem of your night-robe. You press your hand to where your stomach is. The soft swell of it. Where your baby will, please God, soon kick. Where he has touched. You've lived inside your body with this man, and he is being murdered over, over. So much blood. So many juts of bone, white and yellow-grey. The cling of fat. The curve of exposed muscle. The inside of his body spilling out. You cannot watch this over, over, over. The force of it. You grip him tight. His stomach, chest and back. You press your head in.

'You do not have to stay,' he tells you. 'There are horses. Carriages. And money. I would like if I could spare you this. But I cannot. But you can spare yourself. You can away.'

And you are used to facing different pains.

You tell him, 'No.'

He looks at you. His eyes are very sad. His hands upon a bigger, wider door. Another stairs. You leave the cathedral of broken husbands. You leave their pain, but take with you your own. You venture up. The turret that he spoke of. When you came here. Where you could see your home. What was your home.

The night is cold. Your breaths mist soft together. Your head against his chest. You stare at the stars. The mirror-lake. The beetle of the fortress. Your fingers twine. His pulse beats quick as hooves.

You look at him. You think of your six brothers, war-like faces. Your father picking battles. Taking lands. He gives with one hand, weapon in the other. You do not need to ask your husband who. You know. You know. The words pulse in your throat. You do not have the tools to forge them rightly. You look at him. His shoulders straight. He stares. His eyes register no surprise as they appear, six riders. The horizon. His face the face you love. His beard is blue.

You do not have to ask him what he did. You know that it was nothing. There doesn't have to be a reason here. The world will steal what little crumbs you grasp. The loves you have can die and be reborn. The memory of pain will cling. Will cling. And you will never let yourself forget. That this has happened.

You hold his hand. You sense the horse hooves fluttering like wings around the river. Breaths approach the candle of your life. You have no training in the use of weapons. You close your eyes. You feel the tears like pus inside a boil, hot and putrid, churning like a nausea. You love a witch. And when you love a witch, you must prepare. For somebody will come. And they will find that witch. And they will break them. You focus on his bearded, doomed face.

'You will come back,' you say. 'You will come back.'

He tells you that he will. Not right away. And maybe not for years. Your hand in his. You tell him you will wait. That you will stay. You hate to leave the house. You're good at staying. You are good at caring for this man. Your only friend.

Anger laced with love and lancing through you. Feet on stairs, there isn't any way you can prevent this. Someone will always come and always kill him. Find a reason. The only thing that you can do is listen, and stay, and love.

You feel his life. His life upon your hands. The heat of it. The tender weight of blood. Their hands pull you away.

Your heart keeps beating.

Harder than before.

Riverbed

My father married someone beautiful. My mother shone. But shining things attract the grasp of hands. She died when I was very young. I remember her death in colours. The red of blood on sheets. The white of cloth. The soft brown of her skin. It looked too pale, almost the colour of ash. The embers dead. The fire had gone out.

All witches burn.

My father found my mother floating, happy, in a forest river. Like a pretty leaf, a shining stone. He took her home, back to his castle, village.

And she spoke to Him the way that no-one could. He loved her for it, loved her forthright ways. She insisted on nursing me herself. This was unusual. They want their children to

taste other people right away here. But I did not. I am their
only child.

My mother slept curled up in a little ball, the sheets packed
around her. Like a pearl in an oyster. A hazelnut encased inside
a shell. I remember her in things she looked like. My plump
little hand and her large one, stroking the soft grey hair of a
donkey in the stables. The *hmmph* noises they make, these
angry, tender beasts we both enjoyed.

There is a soft rebellion to a donkey. It is a working thing.
But it resents. I am fond of this. When I am cold or lonely in
the castle. When I'm afraid, I often find myself around the
stables, stroking them as long as they permit. Which is a goodly
time. They trust me now. I earned it. Growing up, and being
gentle, kind.

I stretch beneath the sky. The moon is high. I look like her,
they say.

It terrifies me.

Sometimes burdens can make people stronger. And sometimes, people break under the weight. My father, peace be with
Him, snapped like a twig when mother died. I've never known
Him the same. The kingdom is run by His advisors. And they
are greedy men. My father is a greedy man as well, but not for
money. He is greedy for beautiful things. Jewels, pieces of art.
Local girls from villages and townships. He brings them here,
and pays them when they leave. Sometimes people whisper that
He will marry again. That He has found a new bride. Floating
in the water, in the woods.

I hide my face. When I go to Him I hide my face. I smear dirt on it, cut my skin and rat my hair as wild as it can go. Wrap a veil around my mouth, my nose. Poke fingers in my eyes to keep them bloodshot. The features that I wear are hers. They're hers, you see. And He can never know. Or He will have me.

He has vowed that He, blessed be His name, will only wed when He meets someone as lovely as His wife was. I was thirteen the first time that I saw Him look at me. The way that men look at women. My lady saw it too, she spirited me away. We walked together, outside of the castle where there are no secrets, towards the stables. She placed me on my donkey's back. She led it to the river, in the woods. The place He found her. And she told me this.

My father's vow.

May God smile on Him, He had a broken heart. I understand. Half His heart is gone, may He reign for a thousand years, and He is looking for it. When my mother died, He wailed and screamed. He rent His clothes, tore out His golden beard. It grew back white. He had a broken heart. He made a vow. That He would only marry if He met a woman with my mother's face again.

'He will marry you,' my lady told me. 'He will take you to His bed. He will lock you up inside a room. He will stare at you as though you were a fruit for Him to eat. You will grow pale. And you will waste away. Food will not taste like food. You will be lonely. You will grow His children in your womb. And you will love them, and He will be jealous of that love. His fists will black your eyes. And you will try to go back to the place you came from. But the child's small hands will hold you here. A little link, a shining golden chain. You need to go,' she told me. 'You need to flee. As soon as you can. Find a place where you can hide. And hide there. Don't come back.' Her face was pale. She touched me with her hands.

I want a life.

Some time has passed. I have been stealing gold. Gathering it in little bags. Burying it in places I remember. And some that I cannot. It's hard to get the time. I love this kingdom but I have her face. More people see that now. I cannot hide for ever. But I need to venture far away. So far they cannot find me. Even further.

She floated down the river, and He found her. Where was my mother from? Who were her people? People tell me that they do not know. But there is something just behind the eyes. I have a sense.

I stroke the soft hide of the donkey in the stables. And I whisper my truths to him, not with my voice in case of ears, but with my touch. Skin to skin contains a sort of truth. A sort of comfort. My father, may He never know want, wants to take me to His bed. Get heirs on me. Shackle me to Him. I wish that He would die. I'd rule this place. I love my kingdom. It is hard to leave.

I wake during the night. He's in my room. I close my eyes. He stays there for a long time. I hear His breath. The flicker of His candle near my bed. And He has seen my face. He knows.

He knows. My heart behind my teeth and I'm afraid. I need to leave this place. I need to go.

In the morning the door won't open when I wake up. My lady brings me water and a dress. It is as golden as the sunrise. The cloth is heavy. Pulling at my waist. Low upon the bosom. She buttons up my shoes. I cannot walk in them. I only mince. One tiny step after another. Bent in two. My feet are bent in two. My face is clean. My hair is oiled and braided. The way that she wore hers. I need to leave. The river out the window shining grey. A ribbon through the village, through the forest. Up the mountains. The grass. The exposed stone. There are caves there. Places you could hide.

The water here begins up in the mountains. It flows into the ocean. I think of water flowing. You can remove a cup. Another cup. And it will still be there. You can block it, but that makes it rise. There isn't any way to stop the water. It's not like life. It isn't like my life. In the throne room, my father, may He live long and beget many sons (but not on me, please God), takes my hand. He smiles out to the crowd.

I am not her. I have a different heart. I do not love Him.

If there were more of me … My hair coiled back from my/her face exposed, exposed, exposed. He looks at me and smiles. The gods have smiled on Him. His hands upon my face. I never once remember Him holding me as a child. It was always servants or my mother. He offers me a goblet and I drink. He smiles at me. He hasn't got as many teeth as I have. They are wide. Like tiles from a mosaic.

Their love, my lady said. It wasn't love. It looked like something else. A sort of hate. A fire that consumed Him.

Witches burn, and sometimes men catch fire. My mother read the cards. She knew her fate. Our hands upon the deck. Mine small, hers bigger. The future isn't written, till you write it.

I will not wed Him. I will not be a queen. Or not like this. I venture down to the stables. Take the donkey for a walk. Three soldiers follow me. Their eyes don't meet mine. Everybody knows. Inside the castle. What will happen. And that it is wrong.

He is our king, may He prosper and be in health. May He forget my face. And may He rot. My eyes sting but I do not cry. I will not give them tears. I am a princess and I tilt my face towards the light above. Sun dapples on the water as it flows. The little silver fish flick through, flick through. And there are secrets written in the world. If only we divine them. Kings' blood flows in me, and witch blood too. I will not yield. My hand upon the fat soft hairy belly. The velvet nostrils tensing and relaxing. Blood pulses underneath his donkey-skin. He crops the wet grass slowly.

If I could swap my body with a dumb beast's ... then what my father wants would still be wrong. I gather up my stupid, heavy skirts, and stride back to the castle. Up the stairs, the doors and gates that part like legs before me.

I look at Him. I say, 'I will not have you. I do not consent.' I say it before everyone. The courtiers. The servants and the soldiers. My father, all grace abound towards Him, meets my eyes. He simply doesn't care. I run my nails across my arms. They are short, but I can make them draw blood. If He continues this, I'll rend my hair. I will gouge at my skin. Pull out my teeth. I will not look like her. Not any more.

I do not scream. I simply state the facts. I'm taken to my room. They bind my hands and feet. I'm there for hours. They cannot bind my brain. And I am thinking. Thinking till I sleep. The soft grey skin, the sturdy beating heart. My hands, her hands. The river.

There is a secret there. There is a something I cannot decipher. And my father, may He know peace and wisdom, tantrums like a child for want of me. A servant comes in to wash my face. Her features strong. She cleanses me and paints me, so I please Him. He ventures in. Unties my hand, and tries to cram a golden ring on it. It will not pass the knuckle. Not without a layer of flesh from bone. My mother's face is mine. My hands are His. There is a kingly power in me yet. I stare at Him and tell him I won't have Him.

And He leaves.

I am on my bed for several days. Servants come to wash me of my waste. To spoon weak pap into my angry mouth. I keep on speaking to them. Telling them that it's a sin. The thing my father wants. It is a sin.

A king is free of sin, they tell me. God speaks to Him, they say. I need to do my duty. The third night comes and they remove my blanket. The fifth night comes.

My blanket is replaced. My donkey's skin. The soft grey pelt now only smells of death. I heard him from my window. Being flayed. He was alive. My donkey was alive. They took his skin. He died that night, a servant tells me later. In hushed tones. She wipes the streaks of rage from my cold face.

I am a princess born of king and witch. I won't be treated thus. My mother's hands upon the donkey, cards. His hands on hers. The river flowing and the fire dead. 'Untie me,' I command them. 'I would speak to my father, may He never know hunger or thirst.'

And so I'm oiled and coiffed and dressed again. A dress as pale and pretty as the moon. It's almost bridal. Silk. And He will like that. I smile at Him. I bat my mother's eyes. I am compliant. I tell Him I would get to know Him better. Would dine with Him. Would dance. Would hear Him speak of my mother, so I can learn to better try to please Him. He twirls me round. His lips upon my cheeks are old and wet. They smell of death. The dead skin of my donkey folded up. It rests beneath my mattress. It reminds.

My dress is like the moon. I have a month. The cycle of a moon. And then there'll be a wedding. He smiles at me, and thinks that He is charming. His face is mottled. The servants open up my mother's chambers. Her window looks upon the river bend. The forest and the mountains. The soldier behind me keeps his hands upon his sword the entire time. I find her cards. A singing bowl. A mirror. I take them back with me. I look and look. My small hands. Her big ones. His fingers pushing gold onto my skin. It doesn't fit. It hurts. It isn't right.

'Do you have a daughter?' I ask the soldier. He inclines his head. 'And would you marry her?'

He doesn't move. The question is a trap. Everything I say and all I do. A trap for men. I am a trap for men. I rub my hands across my face. My father, may the sun smile upon Him, thinks that He is being kind. He could force me in a different way. This isn't kindness. It isn't a reprieve.

My face, my mother's face, is still too lovely. I watch it in the mirror, grim and drawn. The singing bowl with river-water in it. The cards splayed on the table. Every time, I read a different future. The Fool. The King. The Jack. The Mouth. The Rooster.

The King. The Mouth. The Fool.

The King.

The Mouth.

The King. The Fool. The Mouth.

I run the mallet all around the rim. Until it screams. The edges of the bowl are carved with leaves and water. Fish and flowers. They took his skin while he was still alive. And now he's dead. This kingdom is my home. My father, may His reign be long and just, shaves it from me, piece by piece. Until I am a naked, pleading thing, depending on His pleasure and His love. That won't be me. I won't let it be me.

I coil my hair atop my head, as though it were a crown all by itself. When He marries me, I'll be the queen. But not the sort of queen that has a voice. The bowl sings higher. I look down at the water. And I wonder. There are places women can escape to. Away. Away. And one of them is death.

I ask the king, may He know life eternal, to show me the place He first met my mother. I want, I say, to better understand the love He felt. I take Him by the hand. It is the first touch of my own free will. He looks at me. His eyes are almost kind. They shine with hope. We ride on polished horses, tall and proud. I think of the sturdy little back of my donkey. The grumpy trot, the churlish toss of head. The rough grey hair.

I love the forest. Breathe the air. I wish He wasn't here. I wish that I could be a child again. Curl inside my mother's womb, a walnut in a shell. Divide into two things and not be born. I wish she'd never had to meet this man.

I swallow down such thoughts. They are not meet. I am a princess and a ruler born. And I will bear my burden with quiet grace. His horse pulls up. It's golden like His beard was. His teeth flash at me, yellowing and long against the gum. I allow Him to help me dismount. His hand upon my waist, upon my back. I do not protest His eager touch.

The soldiers watch. I walk towards the river. Leaves kiss the silver surface of the flow.

'She floated to you on the river?' I ask. 'How did she look?' His avid tongue describes in perfect detail. The gleam upon the treasure He once owned.

'I would look like that,' I say, 'for you. We can begin again.'

I lower my two eyes. They kiss the soft grass of the forest floor. Where loving teeth once cropped. There are certain things you cannot fight. A witch may burn. But sometimes she must drown. He looks at me. The dawn upon His face is bright indeed. Life flows into the corpse He was. He likes to win, I think. It is a quality His daughter shares. But only one of us is now a king.

I step onto the soft, cool riverbed. Feel mud between my toes. See the pale brown and small silver bodies of the fish flicker by like hidden candle flame. I lie down perfectly. Release the tension in my shoulders, body. I feel myself begin to float. To rise. He stares at me, for the longest time. I smile to Him. I ask Him who He is, and will He join me. A young man's features play about His face. My father nods. His boots squelch in the muck. His cloak removed by soldiers on the bank. They hold His crown and cloak, His gloves and sword. He lies beside me. And I look at Him.

And then I strike.

When I return to the castle, water drips along the marble floor. Servants hasten to wipe it up. I meet with His advisors and I tell them what has happened. The soldiers on the banks incline their heads. His men agree with me. My ageing father turned into a fish, He swam away. 'We all know of the witchcraft in the woods,' I tell the nobles. They incline their heads. We all incline our heads.

'He would, of course,' I say, 'want me to rule in His stead. Until He can return, God keep Him well.'

'God keep Him well,' they say.

A crown upon my head. My ringless hands hold all their futures now. My brain is humming, singing like a bowl with all before me. The things I could enact. The change. The mountains curl like friends around the castle. I remove the tight braids from my hair. I set it free. I rub my aching scalp. I get to ruling.

Taxes. Bargains. Peace. I bid them make my donkey-skin a cloak. I wear it on the throne. I do a man's job with a woman's face. A witch's heart. A witch can burn. A witch can flake to ash. Can drown a king.

My mother's face and mine. Her hand on my hand. The two of us together. Ageing bones in water, silt and rock. Both their deaths recalled in different colours. Red and Brown and White. Gold and Grey and Blue and Green.

And Black.

The Little Gift

The river is deep. And it is taking me towards the ocean. Away from everything I've ever known.

I was born inside the castle walls. Have never been so far away before. It is unsettling. I don't know who my father is, not really. He caught my mother when she was fifteen. Her first week in the castle. My hair is brown and straight. My skin is freckled from the sun, hands chapped and coarse from work. From early on, I kept the princess company. My mother nursed us both. A queen does not.

We were children raised within the castle, close together. When she was scared of the dark, I slept at the foot of her bed, like a loyal hound. I was whipped for her sins, and for my own. My little hand held tight against a brazier. The sizzle of my flesh. They made her look. And I would see her eyes, so guilty-fascinated. Before she slept, she'd ask me what I felt. She'd hold my hand, or look upon my back. Trace fingers on it. Scratch at little scabs or dried-up blood.

When we were weaned, my mother worked in the kitchens. Chopped and plucked and stuffed and carved and roasted. I saw her less and less. I craved her more. Her tongue was sharp and her eyes were sad, but sometimes she would take me in her arms and she would tell me it was not my fault. What I was. She would tell me to be careful around menfolk. *Never be alone in a room with a man. Never bend over to tie a shoe or to pick something up. You must crouch down. Pretend you are a shadow, or a crab.*

I nodded but I did not know what she meant. I was to learn.

The princess and I, together. An adventure. She will meet her husband. I, my work. She murmurs something quietly to her horse. He murmurs back. They understand each other. I see her shoulders straight. Her golden hair. This prince, I hope that he will be a kind man. I hope he will be worthy of this girl.

We are both in riding cloaks and, underneath, in the same simple dress. Two girls. One gilded and one dull. Until our lives begin again quite differently. I do not know what is in store for me. If I'm to be her maid or in the kitchens. The other servants will not like my voice, my 'haughty tone'. Sometimes I hate it too. It brands me. I know that I should tolerate my lot. Many have it worse. The princess rats at the note from her mother in her pocket. A letter full of protocol and rules.

'I can't abide it, Rilla,' she tells me.

I make a non-committal little sound.

She rolls her eyes. 'Don't be so servile, always. We're alone.'

'I am a servant, after all. Your Highness.'

'Yes,' she says. 'Yes, I suppose you are.' Her voice is gruff. She has a low voice for a little woman. There is a husk to it. A honeyed heft. When she speaks, people listen. And when she sings. Well – that is something special.

It's not that bad, the journey twixt the kingdoms. Sun dapples on our hair. The river hums. The birds are calling out. Protecting all their little forest patches. *It's mine. It's mine,* they say. I wish I knew what it would be, to cry that out with certainty. I wish that I had something that was mine.

She turns to smile at me. I crook my lips. Her eyes are wide, her mouth is orange–pink. A little cloud at sunrise. It is soft. I know that it is soft. I've daubed that mouth with colour. Her eyes are small, but wide. Lined round with kohl. Her eyebrows darker than her golden hair. Her lashes long. I could paint a portrait of her with my thoughts, could draw the shape of her in the air with my two hands. I've touched her daily, often. Her fine waist under velvet, satin, lace. The proud square of her shoulders draped in ermine. Her hair so gold it tarnishes her crown.

When we were small, we used to play at being from the village. We would be two village girls. Two sisters. Our father would be a butcher because my princess loves meat. She wouldn't want to give it up for anything. Our mother would be a seamstress because she loves fine clothes. And we would run and play. She could not afford to get her dress dirty, so she would remove it. And I would do so too, because she asked. I loved to keep her company. She has this smile. It only shows the top half of her teeth. There is a tiny gap between the front two. Some women in the castle use little sticks to force their teeth apart to effect the same thing. People can be stupid.

I can be stupid. I swallow down my feelings. We're not friends. And we were never sisters. When they found us out, they opened up my back. I bear the scars. A river on my skin. Dashes atop dashes. They are old. You don't forget the pain. It teaches you. I do not think I learned the things they wanted, though. I learned to hide. To hate. To do my job and keep my head down. Simmer in a mask. Each small adventure always ends in pain. Needles under fingernails. Fists to face. There is no end of hurts that can be visited on the powerless. I tried to do my best. It didn't work.

Lessons learned. When she speaks to me, I say 'Your Highness', 'Princess' or 'My Princess'. I never say her name. The unguarded bit of me expands with each small freedom I allow it. I need to keep it small to keep me safe.

We venture through the countryside, beside the river. There are no soldiers with us. I am her protector. She is mine. There are skills she has that must be practised in secret. Her horse whispers to her. She combs its mane. Its name is Falada. It speaks to her. Only those with noble blood can understand it. I can make out the meaning, certain words. She knows languages, my princess. German. Hindi. French and English. She has been schooled in how to think and speak.

We set up camp. I light a fire, roast a little bird upon a spit. She points to it. She says my name. 'Rilla.' She says it like it's nothing. Like a friend. I do not think that I have any friends. I'm caught between one world and the next. I don't know who I am. I smile at her. When we are on our own, I meet her eyes.

I have two bloods in me.

And they are warring.

'I would have you sit by me,' she tells me. 'No, not there. Move closer.'

'My Princess.'

I do not think that she knows what she does.

And it is wrong.

'Since we were small, you have been like my sister.' She looks at me. 'But you are not my kin.'

She uncrumples the writing from her mother. I read it. There is nothing there of note. *Be safe, my daughter. Apple of my eyes.* That sort of thing. I think that I would like that sort of thing. To have a mother. Mine is long since gone. She found a man who'd have her and moved on. I do not think that he knows that I am. This husband. Even if she could, she wouldn't write.

'Your mother loves you very much,' I say.

She nods. 'Not enough to keep me, it would seem.'

I look at her face in the firelight. She is incandescent. Something else. I fold my flat, chapped hands on my homespun skirt. I close my eyes. She shines too hard to look at. The soft ripples of her hair like honey-water. So golden that a dragon might fly down. Scoop her up and keep her in his hoard. She looks at me. As though I were worth looking at. As though I had a value. Had a worth.

Do what you are told. Speak when spoken to. My fingers twist like fibre into rope. That tight, that hard. I know my place. I know my place. Our feet beside each other. My stockings with the darned, redarned toes. Hers silken. Blue. I wonder what a silken thing would feel like. On my skin. I swallow. The nudge of her skirts to mine. The softest barrier.

'I worry,' she tells me. 'I worry about what I'll have to do. With him. My mother's letter. She did not enter into the specifics. But there are certain things that I have heard.'

I nod. I know what to expect from men. My mother taught me that. First their eyes. And then their hands and mouths. I've never yet been caught. I am a quick and boring little thing. Head down, hair neat, face low. Don't catch their eye. That's sauce. And men will punish sauce. They call it love. When noble people do it to each other. I don't think there's a word for hands on thighs. Eyes on bodies. Grasping. Pressing in to you and grinding, grinding. We do not swap the stories in the night. It's not like other gossip. That sort of thing can ruin your life. It clings to the meat of you. Ink instead of ash. It stains, it stains you. Once it's known, there is no going back.

'I've never kissed a man,' my princess says. She tilts her head to mine.

I think of stable boys grasping handfuls of me, footmen's tongues a-clash against my teeth. I think of *Good girl.* Think of *How you've grown.*

She is like me now, in a way. Her birthright will afford her some protection. But in the end, we're bodies in the dark. Meat approaching meat.

'It's not that bad,' I tell her. 'I don't know much about the other thing. But kissing's not the worst.'

Fat tongues and yellow teeth. My poor princess.

'Have you kissed many people?' she asks me.

I think on it. 'I've never kissed a person,' I tell my princess. 'I have been kissed. It's never been my choice. I've never dared.' It comes out without thinking.

And she is close to me. Twice a day, the sun can almost touch the earth. My skin's awake. Every part of me is on the surface. Her hand against my face. Her blue eyes on my brown ones.

'You are soft,' she tells me. 'I hope my prince is soft.'

Our hands entangled now. Enmeshed together. Her face to mine. Disturbing me. Upsetting all I am. And we are kissing. Several kinds of sin, and all at once. I've never had this wild surfeit of feeling. There was a dam in me. But it has burst. I learn more of her. The sounds she makes. The tremors and the shocks my hands can offer. People die for this. I understand why people die for this. Her hands upon my body soft as down.

In palaces there is always a certain amount of intrigue. Men with servants, ladies and companions, knights and knights. It's unspoken, the things that people do to each other. Secretive and safe. If you speak it aloud, the spell has broken. Naught protects the named. And there are penalties for loving wrong. They'll cut you or they'll burn you or they'll shun you. Make you dance for them in red-hot shoes. Drag you naked through the streets. Shut you in a barrel spiked with glass. Have horses drag your errant limbs apart. But who am I to disobey my own princess?

She smiles at me. We curl together against the warm belly of her horse. Feel the rise and fall of it until we drift. When I wake up, my hand is curled against her stomach. I cup her like an oyster cups a pearl till she wakes up. Her little eyes spark bright for me. The first face that she sees. The love in me is welling up like water. It gathers at my neck. It rises up. I close my eyes. I know that it will drown me. I see my feet encased in white-hot gold. I see the barrel, shining like a geode on the inside. I did not think that I could dare to want this. I did not think at all. I did not dream. Or if I did, I shaped my dreams acceptably. I did not name my wants. I did not know.

My small princess. I brush the hair from off her face. We wash together, splashing in the stream like children do before they learn shame. My shoulders, back, my skin patched bright with water. She smiles at me. I taste her mouth again. Her hands upon my waist and I am lost. I do not know my place.

We have three blissful nights. And then she asks me. To take her place. To be the prince's wife. To wear the treaty pinned against my cloak. To hold the golden cup. To feel his hands upon me in the night.

'I love you.' And her eyes fill up with tears. 'I cannot bear to be with someone else. I cannot bear it.'

And how do you refuse? I hold her and I tell her that I will. I am a servant and she is my mistress. For that, and more than that, I must obey.

A goose, in the right light, can seem a swan. I hold my head much higher than before. I change my voice to match her noble cadence. I have the feeling I would be found out. It's lodged in me, while eating, dancing, feasting. I knew. I knew. Could smell the tang of blood. The singe of flesh. She tells me we will have to kill her talking horse.

'Nobles understand him. And you can't.' She looks at me. Her eyes are desperate. Desperate. Her fingers through his mane. She calls him 'love' and bids a soft goodbye.

I know words to say to make it happen quick. A noble's voice is like a magic spell. You order, they comply. And very quickly. They have been trained, and well. They fear the lash.

His silent head atop a wall beside the stables. *What Comes from Disobedience.* I look at him. He loved her. He was loyal. And now his dead mane hangs. His dead teeth poke from snowy velvet lips. I close my eyes. Such sins I would commit to keep her happy. Such risks I'd take. The two of us felt whole and clean and real. I hadn't had that. Ever, in my life. You understand.

A maid can be a princess very easily. She starts out as my lady's maid. It's nice. Her hands on the nape of my neck as I braid my own hair, apply the paint, pin jewels upon my clothes. Back ramrod straight. We both stand ramrod straight. The confidence of her. It looks like something else. The way she walks with no crown to protect her. Hands and eyes.

I send her to the geese to keep her safe. She won't spend time with adults, only children. She'll have a little cottage of her own. Away from me. But I will try to visit. Golden hair and skin as soft as silk. A thing worth taking. I know that she would fare better far away from people who are used to having things. And so I make that choice for both of us.

Though that is what lets the resentment in. Her lot is harder. I can not do the work. She has to learn, and this takes time and effort. Her hands begin to crack. Her joy diminish. She had thought that serving was a sort of game. I think. A trick that she could play. My gift to her begins to be a burden. And day by day, the weight of it increases. I am not there to soothe her aching shoulders, rub her feet and kiss her freckling face.

I try my best, but I am working too. I play my role.

The castle is difficult in different ways. At nights. He is soft, and fine-faced. Kind in his own way. I do not want him. I submit. I smile. Tell him that I love him. Close my eyes. Conceal my scars, the rush of bitter tears. I think he thinks it noble, my distaste. Too pure and good to love a man and like it. A real princess. If he could only get an heir on me, it could procure my safety. For a time. I know I'll be found out.

A goose can try its best to be a swan. Conceal the ruddy beak, the grating honk. But swans as geese? The air cries out to them. It's not enough. They want clean sheets and gold. The softer life. And when I visit her and stroke her face, I see her clear blue eyes upon my jewels. She does not see their weight, only their lustre. She knows they should be hers. She wants them back.

I really think she loved me. At the start. Without the yoke of servitude upon her. In a soft bed, with warm feet, she could have found it easy to maintain. I tell myself that story in the night. Curl my toes inside a soft, warm bed. Feel dungeon stone approach. The tang of death.

A goose can love a swan. Curled together. Riverweed on rock. And so the narrative was warped and woven, slowly over months. She stopped her smiling when she saw my face. She called me 'Your Highness' without a little tickle to her voice. She crafted a way out of where she was. A swift escape. I let my new maids tend my face and hair with expert hands. I wish someone was there to issue orders. To tell me what to do. To ease my fate.

Little by little, till she tells the stove in her cottage. She could not speak directly to the king 'for reasons of timidity', and so he must press his ear where pipe turns vent. He crouches and he waits there, wrapped in velvet for her pretty mouth to tell her tale. She says that I imposed this life of toil upon her. She will not tell the lie to the king's face. He needs to listen in. She gives me that. A warped sort of loyalty, but it's something. She will not tie the rope. Or wield the axe.

She tells the stove the tale of how I schemed for jewels and castles. Forgot my station. Threatened her with such a range of hurts she held her tongue. The story woven through the castle. She stared upon her geese, upon the lake and built her lies so tall they were the truth. She combs her hair. Tells stories to the walls. She saves herself.

I wanted so to be the one who did that. Who saved my princess from a dreadful fate. I love her still.

One afternoon, I'm called into the throne room. And she is there, in finer clothes than servants get to wear. I know, before he speaks to me, what will come to pass. A servant's skill. We learn to read our masters early on. If we are to survive inside their world. My small hand to the brazier. Her blue eyes. I've hurt for her since I was very small. And why should that change now?

I gaze at her.

My princess. She will not meet my eyes. Won't look at me. I think of her soft fingers on her horse's mane. His desperate corpse eyes high atop the wall.

The prince looks shocked and filled with mild disgust. I glare at him. My body is the same as other bodies. I am not more dirty, or more clean. I hold my stomach, wondering if I can plead my belly.

He bids me choose my punishment, the king.

But I can see my cold death in his face.

The river on my back. Her cold blue eyes. His booming, kingly voice.

'What should be done to servants who usurp their master's place?' he booms his voice across the room to me. Issuing a different sort of order. I square my shoulders, arch my spine. I know, as surely as I know my name, that they mean me. I think of shoes heated to the colour of the sunrise, melting flesh from off my bones. The barrel, filled with jewel-coloured glass. I think of all the things that can be done. To hurt a person. I look at him as though I were a queen.

And when I answer, I use my own voice.

'Why, sir. They should be punished.'

He bids me tell him how. My regal voice carries through the court. She gasps so softly as I shape the words. I can still make her gasp, so, after all. And they all know. I see it in their eyes that they all know.

The first night I arrived, I brushed out my hair, and found some gold strands tangled with my own. As close as close can be. My rough hands tried to hold her. And they failed. I swallow down my hopes. My wings are hobbled, plucked. And I am flightless.

I spend some time inside his royal dungeons. Learning lessons I've been taught before. And then it comes.

They weigh me down with iron and with gold. Sewn into my shift. My hair brushed bright. The prince glares at me. My common body sullying his own. She steps into the room, and holds his hand. Her eyes cast down. She will not look at me.

Reach out your hand, I think. *And touch my hair. Please give me that, at least.*

I am not a servant or a princess. I am a person just about to die. To die for love. I look at her. I knew just what she was. I knew the risks. And yet I ventured in. 'From her own lips,' a courtier proclaims, 'she chose her fate.'

And isn't that what every woman wants?

He reads my words.

I have been written down. I'll be remembered. That is something surely. To be in words. To be a life in words.

'One such as that should be taken down to the river. In regal garments, lined with little precious weights. And they should venture in, and there remain until their life is lost. Their body should be left there. To the fish.'

Her blue eyes on my skin. Her fingers traced my scars beside the river.

My hair is loose. It whips against my face. My heavy garments pull my shoulders down. Iron and gold.

The weight of two girls kissing.

And she is there, her golden hair and skin as soft as down. I feel her hungry eyes on my cold body. Wind pierces through the cambric of my robe.

I hold my head up high.

I am a person and I have a value.

I know love. I shine that love at her. She meets my eye. I see the lies she's woven pull soft apart.

A little 'Oh' and then her mouth shuts tight. I venture in. One foot in front of the other. The current claims me down, and down and down.

The river is deep. And it is taking me towards the ocean. Away from everything I've ever known.

Beauty and the Board

In the dark confines of a cold place, a girl opens the cloth that wraps the board.

She takes the planchette out. It is shaped like a heart. There is a monocle in the centre. A little disc of glass. She presses her finger to the smudge of it. To all the fingers, asking things before. Her hair is long. It hangs, like dead men, down beneath her shoulders. Her dress is white. Her dress is always white. The night is dark. Her eyes are shot with blood, like cracks in tile. She has been so tired and for so long. The scrape of stone beneath her. Little sounds of people doing things. The night is busy here. It's always busy. The walls curve round. The tower walls curve round.

To craft a board like this you must be skilled. It is no little task. It wasn't hers. She got it from her mother. Or she thinks she may have. In a box. A wide and slender box. The soft black leather length of it beneath the furs. Beneath the silk, the lace. She left a box of somethings when she went. Men liked her mother, but of course they liked her. No better than she should be. People knew. The what but not the who. Not all she was.

To grow up in a castle. Like a lady, but not quite a lady. Like a child, but so far from a child. Velvet sheets and jewels and strong perfume. Boxes inlaid with mother-of-pearl. Little runes, protecting what's inside. Silk nightgowns behind screens and night-time sounds. To be a by-blow, worth a sideways glance. If that. Invisible.

She spent her childhood looking at what passed from around corners, or through window panes. She wandered, quite alone. Not all alone.

We are not the only thing that's here.

She knew that young. That there were different sorts of lives. Such different ways to be part of the world. Half-in, half-out. Or working slowly in, sucking at the borders, like a tick. Swelling full of other people's colours. Thirsting for another little sup.

She was fair of face, and kept away. Her mother knew the value and the danger. Of being something people liked to watch.

A child reminds them of disgusting worries. A swollen belly or a milky tit. A pane of glass lowers under the soft globes of their eyes. Like a screen to ward off hungry insects in the night. In case they'd get a taste. The weight of caring switches off inside them. She feels them push away. She doesn't mind. She knows it keeps her safe. This focused unawareness. She knows she still has spirits. And her mam.

For a time, they stick together. Wrapped in pretty fabrics. Big doll, small doll. Feathers in their hair and safe to play with. Painted mouths and pleasing aspects. Hand in little hand. They mind each other. Big one and the small. The bright. The dark. But always there is something dreadful coming. They try to be prepared. They're not prepared.

When she is still a girl, her mother displeases somebody who matters. They wall her up, and her forgotten child becomes a ghost.

Who's that?

The witch's daughter.

That whore they locked away inside a room?

She had a child.

A quiet little creature, scared of people.

Not right in the head.

Ears to the walls, and hides behind the drapes.

The scrape of nail behind the wall – sometimes she hears it. They say it's what remains. It could be rats. She used to place her hand against the flat stones, cold or hot, and wait for something real to filter through. Sometimes she would shiver. Was that love? A mother's ghostly touch?

She grows up pretty, so the people tell her. A compliment. A threat. She doesn't know. They have begun to look. And look again. In her cold bed, with her warm hands, she traces the edges of the mattress. A space alone. A space where she feels safe. It's stuffed with straw. They dress her well; they dress her and they feed her. But still, she knows she isn't one of them.

Sunday morning Mass. The priest kisses the book. Upon the altar is a preserved hand. It belonged to a saint. When he was dead, his lovers cut it off. They took it around and let it out to people. Touch it and be healed. And be redeemed. She knows the book. She touches it. Recites it. She stands up and she kneels. She eats the flesh. She watches wine turn blood. One night, when she wakes up, she is a woman. She doesn't feel that different but she is. She tries to hide it, but the castle knows things. The walls and floors and windows full of eyes. There's hope inside her gut that they will leave her. That time will pass, she'll live, and she will die. She wants to float through life unnoticed always. She wants to be a ghost. A kind of ghost.

In the garden, at the very end of it, there are fish and there are dragonflies on lily-pads. The water's warm. The flora in it tangled. Before long, the fish will start to choke. The green will bloom. She trails her small hand in. The blood under her fingernails calls something. Cold lips at the soft pads of her hands. She feels a shock whisper through her body. Something else. Another ghost like her.

A different thing.

In the nursery, the princes and princesses hatch like eggs. Six golden heads that trundle through the castle. The elder ones are far away. At weddings and at wars. She murmurs prayers as dead mouths kiss her fingers. *The taste of life. Oh, it has been so long!* Her hand is cold for days, waxy cold, and smooth like alabaster. It feels like it is made of different stuff, but looks the same. She cannot see the join of cold to warm. She cannot see a thing. But still she knows.

She lowers her eyes when they approach. It is what's done. The taint of what her mother was upon her. The mother she remembers vibrant, wild. A force for good. A good thing in her life. A clever woman. And she was killed. The way that people are. A little piece at first then all at once. She does not feel ashamed of where she came from. But everything has taught her that she should. She listens to the soft beat of her heart. The pulse of blood. In corridors, if you raise your eyes to meet a man's, there is a chance he'll touch you. She wants to be untouchable. She wants their hands to pass right through her skin and come out raw. She wants some peace. So she obeys their rules. They've taught her well. Her eyes are lowered now. In candle-light. Towards the board. The asking-board. The use of it an art. You can invite things in, into the world. The door is there. She only needs to knock.

When she was smaller, she lived within her mother's apartments. The rooms got smaller as her mother aged. And when the king died, some of her did too. *Your heart chooses a person, and you love them,* her mother told her. *It is an act of faith. It is a choice. You grow it like a seed. And if need be, you take what's grown and kill it. Deprive it of sweet water and your thoughts. You starve it like a prisoner, and do not take it out until you're fairly sure that it is dead. It takes a lot to kill a thing like love,* her mother told her and she gripped the soft flesh of her forearm very tightly, as though her daughter were a cut of meat. *Listen, child,* she said, *this is important. You have his blood. And that gives you a value. A woman with a value is in danger. There is a ticking clock inside your womb.*

And then she showed her daughter what to do. The skills. The calling. *There are other things in the world. They use their god to warp you to their ways. But if there is above, there is below. And you can use the things that live there. They were angels once before they fell. They understand all that the world can be. And if you offer them a juicy treat, they'll offer you protection in return.*

Say the words while curled between two mirrors. Use the board. It will provide responses to your questions. Iron out the details. Like a treaty. Remove your clothes. Carve significant patterns into your skin and let the red make rivers on the floor. Let it flow like tangleweed in questing curlicues and little tendrils. You only ask them when you are in need, when you have tried all else. And so you want them hungry in the room with you. And memory may err. But blood does not.

Hunger blunts and sharpens all at once. She feels the cold inside her hands again. It is the river thing. Her fountain-fiend. It smells like riverbed. Like stale, cold water, fat with rot and sediment and something else she does not have the experience to describe. Perhaps a pike. A fish with many teeth. A hungry creature. Her blood furls into something else's slime. The board

is colder now, the surface of it has begun to give, but just a little. It gives like flesh. It almost seems to breathe.

The girl on the wet floor in her skin. The walls are thick with cold and fluid mist. There's pools of something cold and dark and salty. She doesn't stop to wonder why that is. Her knuckles white as bone, as cold as death. She is a thing with eyes and lips. With hair. A thing with organs, blood. A thing with thoughts. She speaks them in the dark.

'They would have me marry an old man. I do not know him and I do not want him. They say he uses women cruelly. That he likes young flesh. And I am not a thing that can be used.'

The planchette quivers, like a minnow on a hook. She eyes it:

W.E.C.A.N.A.L.L.B.E.U.S.E.D.

The girl runs a finger through her long dark hair. The damp air has infused it, and it is plastered to her soaked skin.

'We can,' she says. 'But I would rather have the use of me.'

The room is warmer now, the air is murky. The letters on the board are hard to see.

W.H.A.T.D.O.Y.O.U.W.A.N.T.W.I.T.H.M.E.

'I know you,' she tells the water-thing. 'I think that I have known you quite a while. My mother taught me love. She taught me rage.'

After the king died, her mother's apartments became smaller still. She still walked straight-backed, proudly through the court.

Until they took even that from her. Until they walled her up to rave and starve. No-one knows exactly the location. The girl has spent years knocking at the walls. Scratching surfaces behind the tapestries. Long after hope was lost the girl had hope. An answer or a body. A grave to visit or a place to look.

S.H.E.D.I.E.D.S.C.R.E.A.M.I.N.G.A.L.O.N.E.

The girl lowers her head and whispers to the board as though it were a friend.

'I know.' She licks her lips, she swallows. 'My mother, though she practised the dark arts, was chained by love. She loved me. And she loved the king, my father. And they are dead. I have nobody now. There isn't space for love in me. I have killed it, slowly over years. I have only hope and only hate. And so, I propose a game of hate and hope.'

The planchette eases slowly over the board, a sea-snail now. There is a trail of ooze between the glyphs.

I.L.I.S.T.E.N.

With her pink mouth and her dark eyes, the girl draws a picture of the man. The one they call the Vulture. With his cruelty and influence. His trail of broken brides. They took the girl into a room. The queen was there. She bid her sign a contract. And there were men. With bricks and mortar too. They bid her choose her fate. The girl chose quietly. And she made the marks. He will come to bring her to his castle. He will hurt her outside and her in. She has heard whispers of the girls before her. Their blood-price paid in bags of golden coins. Decreasing value. What would she be worth in blood and gold?

'I cannot escape,' she tells the mist.

N.O.N.E.C.A.N.

'And so I come to you. I offer you my company. My blood. My mother told me to be careful of the visitors the board could call. To only use it as a last resort.'

The girl's voice softer, speaking of her mother. Metallic tang, the hulls of rusty ships beneath the sea. Old sailor blood. The hint of brine collects around the edges of her nostrils. There is an ocean living in this thing. Its misty breath.

'There is evil in the world as well. And bad as he might be, I would be worse.'

The girl ropes her hair back from her eyes. They flicker around the room, settling on the thickest patch of mist. Fat with scent and almost dense enough to cast a shadow. Her hands never leaving the planchette, she meets the part she thinks might be its gaze.

'I have felt your hungry mouth on me. Since childhood, I have felt the chill of you. You are a thing. A beast without a home. I know that, how it feels. And I would have you share a place in me.'

Again, the board moves, this time softer, smoother, sliding like an eel.

Again, it says,

I . L . I . S . T . E . N .

'Come live in me. A lodger in my body and my brain. And, if the man they've sold me like a pig to lays a hand on me, then venture to the surface. Come and play. Teach him the things the world teaches women. Ensure he learns his lessons very well.'

The board is silent. But the mist is pulsing like a heartbeat, like a breath.

'I know what it is to want a life. I would share mine to keep it.'

E . V . E . N . W . I . T . H . T . H . E . B . E . A . S . T .

'I know my mind. And you will know as well.' The girl smiles. There are certain skills I do not have. You do. And I would have you share them with this ageing thing who seeks to wed with something fresh and soft. I am not a new loaf to be eaten. And if he tries, I would remove his teeth and feed them to him.'

I . L . I . S . T . E . N .

This time it jumps like a dolphin, like a hopeful heart. It wants this. It has wanted this, the girl thinks, for a very long time. She does not wonder if she is sure. The years in isolation weigh on her. She knows her mind. But what would it be like for someone else to know it too?

The girl swallows. 'I am not unafraid of you, Beast. But I have known you since I was a child. I am not a child any more. I am a woman grown. And I am angry.'

I . W . I . L . L . A . C . C . E . P . T . T . H . E . N .

And it is upon her, in her nostrils, through the tiny holes where tears come out. The small bones in her ears are freezing, freezing. And all at once, the room is clean and still and as it was.

The hair has darkened raven-feather-blue. The eyes are paler, flecks of river-water through the brown. The cuts have closed, the skin as smooth as the surface of a liquid. Porcelain and pore-less. They smooth their hands over their new face, and it pleases them. They pick up their white shift, now stained with blood and silt and what has happened. Their white teeth kiss their red lips. A pink tongue tests their strength. Whole, sharp and even. They venture out into the moonlit halls, walking naked through the dangerous places unafraid and wild with cold, bright beauty.

Something in them ticking like a clock. Not just the womb, but fingers, muscles, eyes, poised for battle, glistening with life. The two together. Tale as old as time.

And they are ready.

T H E   E N D

Candle-magic:
bright lights
that made me braver

Writing a book is scary, if you mean it.
These people made the earth solid and the water gentle.

I light candles for you all. I thank you.

S C A R L E T :

Strength, courage, energy, ambition; spark and flame
Little Island – Gráinne and Siobhán (from the very first step) –
for believing in this book and helping it on its way.

W H I T E :

Balance, clarity, divination, exorcism
My agent, Clare Wallace – all of the above, and kindness too

P I N K :

Joy, healing, compassion, caring; loving; being loved
My family – Mam, Dad, Tadhg, Nana; Kings and Sullivans.

BRIGHT ORANGE:

Happiness and enthusiasm

Jacq, Dave, Mary-Brigid, Helen, Vivian, Karina, Lisa, Bob,
Ellen, Cameron, Fidelma, SLARI, Elaina and all at CBI, Jenny,
Shannon, Arianne, Mariam, Sophie, Ciara Ní Bhroin and so
many others – booksellers, librarians, bloggers, YA book-club;
every reader who has gotten in touch or taken the time to
review my work: you remind me to take joy in it, that it's not
just me, inside a room alone

SILVER:

Reflection and truth; intuition

My students, for teaching me

BLACK:

Absorbs all colours; depth, the unconscious, support

Karen Vaughan, who made my words her art – I'm so glad
my stories get to live with and through your gift

YELLOW:

Inspiration, creativity, the sun

Writers who've helped this percolate inside my heart
for years – Angela Carter, Hans Christian Andersen,
Oscar Wilde, Jack Zipes, Marina Warner, Anne Sexton,
Emma Donoghue, Paul Bae, Terri Windling
and Ellen Datlow

GREEN:

The earth; trees and plants and healing

The Doomsburies – Graham Tugwell, Dave Rudden, Sarah Maria Griffin; growing things together is the best

BLUE:

Water; protection and guidance

Claire Hennessy, Sheena Wilkinson, Sarah Crossan, Sinéad Burke, Suzanne Keaveney, Ciara Banks, Camille DeAngelis, Cian Ó Ceallacháin, Danny Golden, Sinéad O'Brien, Sarah Webb, Louise O'Neill, Juno Dawson, Trish Forde, Andi Ludden Reilly, Tara Flynn, Tom Rowley

BROWN:

Grounding, protection of familiars, locating lost objects; protection, special favours, (best) friendship

Diarmuid O'Brien – hearth and heart and home; I don't know what I did or what I'd do

About the author

Deirdre Sullivan is from Galway and is now living in Dublin, where she works as a teacher.

Her hugely acclaimed novel *Needlework* consolidated her reputation as a leading Irish YA author. *Needlework* was shortlisted for the Irish Book Awards and went on to win the Honour Award for Fiction at the Children's Books Ireland Awards in 2017.

Her Primrose Leary series was also widely praised; two of the Prim books were shortlisted for the Children's Books Ireland Awards; and the final one, *Primperfect*, was also short-listed for the European Prize for Literature.

About the illustrator

Karen Vaughan is a designer and illustrator with a particular love for pen and ink. Since receiving her BA in Illustration from The North Wales School of Art and Design at Glyndŵr University in 2013, Karen has worked as a freelance graphic designer and illustrator producing covers, illustrations and designs for numerous publishing companies and newspapers. Her intricate illustrations are very much inspired by folk tales, nature and the elaborate patterns and fashions of bygone eras.

http://kvaughan.com/

About the publisher

Based in Dublin, Little Island Books has been publishing books for children and teenagers since 2010. It is Ireland's only English-language publisher that publishes exclusively for young people. Little Island specialises in publishing new Irish writers and illustrators, and also has a commitment to publishing books in translation.

www.littleisland.ie